BADLANDS
DEATH IN DRYGULCH

ELDRIDGE JAMES

Catnip

For Jack
from Grandpa

CATNIP BOOKS
Published by Catnip Publishing Ltd
14 Greville Street
London
EC1N 8SB

This edition first published 2010

1 3 5 7 9 10 8 6 4 2

Text copyright © Jim Eldridge, 2010
The moral right of the author has been asserted.

Cover photo of Billy Joe by butterworthdesign.com
Additional background photo from iStockphoto

A CIP catalogue record for this book is available from the British Library.

ISBN 978-1-84647-096-7

Printed in Poland

www.catnippublishing.co.uk

CHAPTER 1

It was dark and it was raining. Billy Joe Ford sat outside the saloon on the boardwalk and watched the rain turning the dirt road into mud. He thought about looking for shelter. There was a livery stable at the end of the street with big bales of hay piled up, which would make a warm bed for the night. But if he went there, then how would his pa find him when he came out of the saloon?

He got up and looked through the window. His pa, John Ford, was sitting at a table with four other men playing cards. Cowhands, by the look of them. Money was piled up on the table, but very little in front of his pa. John Ford usually lost at cards, or he cheated. When he lost he got drunk and beat Billy Joe. When he cheated and won, he still got drunk, but on those occasions he didn't beat him. Well, not straightaway. Usually he went off and found a woman, and she'd steal his money from him while he was out cold. John Ford would wake up and find out he'd been robbed, and then he'd beat Billy Joe. Or try to, but usually he was still so drunk he'd miss. It was a hard life, but it could be worse. A boy like Billy Joe could be working in a mine, or in the cotton fields. As it was, he and his pa moved from town to town – John Ford gambling, Billy Joe begging and stealing. It was a job. According to his pa it was the only kind of job Billy Joe would ever get in this land.

'It's cos of you being half-Injun half-Irish,' his pa had told him. 'Now if you'd took after me and looked Irish, you'd be fine. Your trouble is you take after your mother's people, the Comanche. You look too much like an Injun for white people to trust you, but at the same time you look too much like a white boy for the Injuns to trust you. Trust *me*, Billy Joe, being a half-an-half like you are, you ain't got nothing but trouble comin' to you in this life.'

And so far trouble was about all Billy Joe had seen in his eleven years. But most of it had been caused by his pa getting them into difficult situations. Gambling. Getting drunk and starting fights. Messing with other men's women. Cheating at cards.

As Billy Joe looked through the window into the saloon, he saw his pa throw a card down on the table and grin, then lean forward and put his hands on the pile of money in the centre of the table.

As he was pulling the money towards him, one of the other men suddenly reached out and grabbed John Ford's arm and twisted it so a playing card fell out of his sleeve onto the table.

Billy Joe's pa looked shocked, and then he went for his gun. He never made it. The man who'd grabbed his arm pulled out a pistol and shot John Ford twice in the chest. Billy Joe heard the shots through the thick walls of the saloon. He watched as his pa crashed back into his chair, then carried on falling backwards, blood spreading rapidly across his shirt, his arms flailing, his eyes wide in shock. He hit the floor and lay there, his eyes staring straight at Billy Joe.

Billy Joe stood, stuck to the spot, his mouth open in shock. It felt like his heart had stopped and he couldn't breathe. Pa was dead! Killed right in front of his eyes!

Suddenly Billy Joe realized that the cowhand was now aiming his gun straight at him!

He threw himself to one side just in time. There was the explosion of the gun and then the window shattered at the exact spot where his head had been.

There were shouts and screams from both inside and outside the saloon, but Billy Joe was already running as fast as he could, fear and panic driving him on. A gunshot sounded behind him and chips of wood flew up around his feet. He had to get off the boardwalk, but if he ran into the rain-lashed street he'd get stuck in the mud for sure and the gunman would just shoot him dead.

There was another gunshot, and Billy Joe felt this bullet tear at the sleeve of his jacket. The next one would blow him apart!

He reached the end of the boardwalk and threw himself off. He tried to move to the left, heading for the darkness of an alleyway, but mud clung to his boots, holding him. The next second he felt a blow in the back, and then he was face down on the ground.

CHAPTER 2

Billy Joe was being dragged, sliding in the mud, and before he knew what was happening, he was under the boardwalk. A hand was pressed over his mouth to stop him crying out.

'Lay still!' whispered an urgent voice.

There was the sound of running footsteps above on the wooden boardwalk. They drew closer and stopped right above his head. A voice said, 'Forget it, Boone. He was just some kid.'

'He was with that no-good card sharp,' snapped the voice of the man called Boone. 'Maybe he was his kid, or something. I'm just making sure he don't come and shoot me in the back some time.'

'Why would he do that?' demanded another man.

'Revenge,' said Boone, grimly. 'It's what I did to the man who killed my pa. Ain't no one too young to kill someone.'

'That kid didn't look like the killing kind.'

'Everyone's the killing kind. Remember that.'

The firm brutal way Boone said this sent a shiver down Billy Joe's spine. I ain't the killing kind, and nor was my pa! he wanted to shout out. But the hand over his mouth and his own fear kept him quiet.

'Anyways, looks to me like he's long gone,' said one of the other men.

A pause, then a grunt from Boone.

'He's here somewhere. I can smell him,' he said, a note of grim determination in his voice, and Billy Joe tensed up even more.

There was a silence that seemed to last for an eternity then, finally, Boone spat into the street.

'OK,' he grunted. 'We'll leave it for now. But I'll know that boy again. And when I see him, he's dead.'

Then came the sound of boots walking away. The pressure of the hand over Billy Joe's mouth eased off. As his eyes grew accustomed to the darkness, Billy Joe could see who'd grabbed him: a boy not much older than himself.

'Who...?' he began, but the boy silenced him with a finger to his lips.

They lay there in the mud beneath the boardwalk for what seemed like ages, and then Billy Joe's companion said, 'OK. Follow me.'

The boy slid out from beneath the boardwalk and headed into the dark alleyway that ran off the main street, and Billy Joe saw that he was about a head taller than himself. The tall boy headed off and Billy Joe followed. They squelched through the mud of the alley, then took a right turn at the end. By now the rain had eased off.

Billy Joe walked blindly, following the boy. His head was in a whirl. His pa was dead. He was on his own now – except for this boy who'd saved him, whoever he was. Where was he taking him?

They turned into a tiny back alley, with just a few derelict houses. There was the dim glimmer of a light shining in one of them. The tall boy headed for this one, unlatched a door and gestured for Billy Joe to step in.

'Welcome to the refuge,' he said.

CHAPTER 3

The lighting inside came from oil lamps. As Billy Joe adjusted his eyes to the dim light, he saw that there were another three boys inside the one-room shack. They had been sitting down but now they were all standing, watching Billy Joe warily.

'This here's a stray,' announced the tall boy. 'I found him out on the street, with a fella chasing him set on shootin' him.'

'He that gambler's kid?' asked one of the other boys.

'Yep,' said the tall boy. He turned to Billy Joe. 'Guess it'd be a good idea to get introduced. My name's Jess.'

Now Billy Joe saw Jess properly for the first time. He was tall and thin with dark hair parted in the middle and hanging down over his ears. He wore a black coat with dark trousers and boots, all covered with mud from the street.

Gesturing at the other boys, Jess said, 'The real

small one is Andy. That tall one there is Pete. Next to him is Shane. They're brothers.'

Billy Joe nodded to the boys.

'My name's Billy Joe Ford,' he told them.

'Hi, B-B-Billy Joe,' stammered Shane, giving Billy Joe a friendly grin.

His older brother, Pete, didn't say anything, just looked at Billy Joe with suspicion in his eyes. Pete looked to be about the same age as Billy Joe but even thinner. His clothes hung on him like they were originally meant for someone much bigger and there were patches of different coloured materials where his clothes had been mended.

Shane looked the friendlier of the brothers. He was shorter but stockier, with broad muscular shoulders that filled his light brown buckskin jacket. Billy Joe guessed Shane was about nine. He noticed Shane's nose went to one side, like he'd been kicked or punched in the face and had his nose badly broken and his brother had a scar on one side of his face. These two had obviously seen their share of troubles.

'What happened out there?' asked the littlest boy, Andy, eagerly. 'You're all covered in mud!'

Andy was real small and looked to Billy Joe like he couldn't be more than six years old. He wore blue dungarees that had definitely been made for someone much bigger, and were now cut down for him. The ends of the cuffs were ragged and the dungarees had been tied around the waist with string to stop them falling down.

'Billy Joe's pa got shot,' explained Jess. 'The fella who shot him seemed set on shooting Billy Joe as well, so we hid under the boardwalk.'

'I guess they caught the guy cheating at cards,' grunted Pete.

'No they did not!' retorted Billy Joe angrily. He knew it was true, but he didn't like the fact that this boy was saying rotten things about his father.

Shane and Andy exchanged puzzled glances.

'Then w-w-why'd they shoot him?' asked Shane.

Pete looked at Billy Joe, his mocking expression challenging him to tell the truth. Billy Joe glared back at him and said nothing, just scowled. OK, so Jess had saved his life, but that didn't mean he had to take these insults.

'I think it'd be a good idea to get out of those wet clothes,' said Jess, and Billy Joe realized that he was intervening, carefully stopping any trouble before it started. 'We can hang 'em to dry by the stove.'

'I ain't staying,' said Billy Joe. 'I got to get out of town before that man finds me.'

'He won't find you here,' Jess assured him. 'And if you go out in the street like that, he'll find you for sure. That, or you'll catch a fever in those wet clothes.'

Jess began to take off his own jacket and trousers, and hung them on a chair near the stove.

For the first time, Billy Joe looked around the room and saw it properly. Although the wooden walls sloped dangerously and the tin roof looked like it had holes at the corners, an attempt had been made to make the shack look reasonably comfortable. Curtains and drapes hung from the ceiling down the walls. Billy Joe guessed they were there to keep out the draughts as much as brighten the place up.

A wood-burning stove was in the centre of the room, its black chimney pipe going up and through the tin roof. A small fire was burning in it now, glowing red and sending a warm glow around the room.

Billy Joe looked across at Pete, ready for the next insult. Instead, Pete shrugged.

'We ain't got any spare clothes,' said Pete, 'but you can wrap yourself in a blanket.'

With that, Pete picked up a blanket from the floor and gave it to Billy Joe.

Billy Joe hesitated, then nodded.

'Thanks,' he said.

So Jess, the eldest and the tallest, is the leader, he said to himself. *What Jess says, goes. Pete may not like it, but he accepts it. The younger two, Shane and Andy, go along with whatever Jess says.*

Billy Joe took off his own outer clothes and hung them by Jess's near the stove. Then he wrapped the blanket around him. As he did so, Billy Joe saw a large black and white dog sleeping on the ground near the stove, and realized it had previously been hidden by the blanket.

'This is a dog's blanket?' he said indignantly, and began to take it off.

'I'd leave it on if I was you,' said Pete. 'It's better than getting cold!'

'I ain't wearing no dog blanket,' said Billy Joe crossly. 'He could have fleas!'

'Of course he's got fleas,' piped up Andy. 'He's a dog. We all got fleas.'

'No we ain't,' said Jess. He gave Billy Joe a friendly smile. 'They're just joshin' with you, Billy Joe. Patch ain't got fleas.' Then he thought about it, and admitted, 'Well, not many. He always gives himself a good scratching. When he wakes up, that is. He's a good watchdog.'

Billy Joe looked down at the sleeping dog, seeing its sides rise and fall as it breathed in its sleep. He even heard it snore.

'If he's so good a watchdog, why's he still asleep?' he demanded. 'I could be anyone walking in here.'

'It's cos he don't feel like being a watchdog today,' said Andy defensively. 'But some days he can be real fierce and growl.'

'He came with the shack,' explained Jess. 'He was living here when I moved in, so I fed him.'

'Another stray?' asked Billy Joe.

Jess nodded, smiling.

'You know, you loo-loo-look like an Indian in that blanket,' grinned Shane.

'No I don't!' Billy Joe snapped back angrily.

Suddenly there was the sound of a sharp knocking at the door and the boys froze.

'They've followed me!' whispered Billy Joe, shocked.

A voice from outside called, 'It's Sheriff Nolan! Open up!'

Billy Joe shrank away even further from the door.

'It's the Sheriff! He's gonna arrest me!'

Jess shook his head.

'Nope,' he said, walking to the door. 'The Sheriff's a good man.'

Jess opened the door and a tall man stepped into the house. He wore the clothes of a cowboy, but a tin star was pinned to his shirt. Two Colt 45s hung from the gun belt around his waist.

'Evening, Jess,' he said. He looked around at the others. 'Evening, boys.'

'Evening, Sheriff,' chorused the boys.

'How can we help you, Sheriff?' asked Jess.

'It seems there was a spot of bother at the Golden Dollar saloon tonight,' said Nolan. 'A man got shot and killed during an argument over a game of cards.'

Jess gave a sigh.

'Cards is sure an unlucky game,' he commented, ruefully. Billy Joe said nothing.

'It was for this man,' said Nolan. 'Now some eye-witnesses said the man who got shot had a boy with him – may have been the man's son.'

Billy Joe felt sick to his stomach. The Sheriff was going to arrest him after all! Maybe force him to be a witness! He shuffled further back out of the light from the oil lamps, doing his best to try and hide behind the other boys. The last thing he wanted was to face the killer, Boone.

If Sheriff Nolan saw Billy Joe moving at the back of the crowd of boys, he didn't say anything. Instead, he said, 'Now *if* there was a boy...'

'We ain't seen him!' said Andy quickly.

Nolan smiled. 'No, of course you ain't, Andy,' he said. 'But if you do, it might be friendly to pass on a word of advice to him. Tell him it might be best for him to get out of town soon as he can. Say, at first light tomorrow. After he'd spent a night somewhere safe, where he could grab a bite to eat and get a bit of sleep.

'The men who were in that saloon tonight look to be a tough and dangerous crowd. I'd hate that boy to run into them again.'

'Yes, sir, Sheriff,' nodded Jess. 'If we see that boy, we'll surely tell him.'

'Good,' nodded Nolan. He reached into his pocket and pulled out a quarter, which he tossed to Jess. 'If you see him, give him this. I'm guessing he ain't got no money and I'd sure hate to see him get in trouble stealing some.'

Jess held the quarter in his hand and hesitated, as if he was going to refuse it. Then he nodded.

'Thanks, Sheriff,' he said. 'We'll pay you back.'

'I know you will, Jess, you always do,' said Nolan. 'But there's no rush.'

'We don't like taking charity.'

'It's not charity. It's a loan.'

With that, he looked round at the boys and tipped his hat to them and Billy Joe could have sworn that as he looked at him, the Sheriff winked.

'Good night, boys. Keep safe.'

With that, Nolan left.

As soon as the door was shut, Jess tossed the quarter to the astonished Billy Joe, who pocketed it.

'Why'd he do that?' asked Billy Joe, stunned.

'Like I said, the Sheriff's a good man,' said Jess. 'He knows we live right and don't cause him nor anyone else no trouble. We don't steal. We don't beg. We don't mess up other people. Any money or food we get, we work for. We clean out the livery stables. We help the blacksmith. We do anything that's honest. That way the people in this town know we're OK and they don't trouble us or try and put us in some kind of home.'

Billy Joe shook his head.

'I never heard of such a thing before,' he said. 'All the towns I've ever been in, the Sheriff was as big a crook as the outlaws he was supposed to stop.'

'That's why we're lucky to have Sheriff Nolan here in Drygulch,' said Pete.

'Come on,' said Jess. 'Let's get some food inside you and get you bedded down for the night. We gotta get you out of town first thing in the morning.'

CHAPTER 4

Billy Joe found sleep difficult to come that night. When he did he was assailed by visions of his father being shot dead in the saloon and himself being chased by Boone. Thick mud in the road was clinging to his feet, holding him, stopping him running, while all the time the gunman was getting nearer and nearer to him.

The nightmare woke him up, covered in a cold sweat.

Awake, Billy Joe lay in the one-room shack listening to the other boys snoring and whistling in their sleep, the sounds of their breathing mixing with that of Patch. Billy Joe felt strange. He could tell these four boys were on their own, no parents to take care of them. Now he was like them. Just a few hours ago he'd had a father. OK, John Ford hadn't been much of a father, but he was the only one Billy Joe had. Now he had none at all.

From his very short acquaintance with them, it seemed to Billy Joe that all these boys had suffered somehow in their short lives, and they all bore the marks of it. Just like he did.

Suddenly he found he was trembling. At first he thought it was from cold, but the blanket and the warmth from the stove told him it wasn't cold that made him shiver. Was it fear? Fear of Boone? Or was it just shock?

In his life Billy Joe had seen many men killed, most of them shot, but the shooting of his father had left him reeling. His pa had been the only certain thing in his life. The beatings, the drunkenness, the women, the card cheating, they'd been things he could almost set a clock by. Or, at least, a calendar. They would return regular as the seasons. Now they had gone, vanished in a moment, gone in the time it took for Boone to pull a trigger. For the first time in his life, Billy Joe was properly alone.

He looked around at the boys and the dog as they slept. The oil lamps had been turned out, but the glow from the stove was enough for him to see the place. He wondered who these boys were? How come they were all on their own? Had their fathers been killed too? If so, what had happened? What had happened to their mothers? How had they come by this shack that they'd made home?

Billy Joe noticed that the thickest blankets had

been put on the smallest boy, Andy, who slept next to the dog. Jess had the thinnest blanket on him, with his coat laid on top of that.

That was the way it seemed to work with this small gang – Pete looked after his younger brother, Shane, Andy looked after Patch the dog and Jess took care of all of them.

This was all alien to Billy Joe. In all his life he'd never had anybody who he could really call a friend. He didn't remember anything at all about the first year of his life. He'd been told by his pa that he'd been born in an Indian village because his pa had been living with the Comanche at that time. John Ford had never told Billy Joe why he had been living with the Comanche, or who his mother was. He'd told Billy Joe she'd been the daughter of a chief, but he never said which one.

He vaguely remembered his mother, but not in the Indian village. It had been afterwards. He and his pa and his mother in some town. And then his mother was no longer around. She'd just vanished from their lives.

Billy Joe didn't know if she'd died or run off. He'd tried asking his pa about her, but every time he did, his pa got angry and hit him and told him to shut up. He wouldn't even tell Billy Joe why she'd gone. All Billy Joe knew was that she had been a Comanche, and he looked like her, at least, enough to annoy John Ford.

It was a big hole in his life. And now, with John Ford dead, he'd never know the answers to the many questions he had about her.

Billy Joe lay there a long while, listening to the sounds of the sleeping boys and the creaking of the wooden walls and the tin roof of the shack, and thought about what he was going to do now. Where was he going to go? One thing was sure, with the man Boone looking for him, he couldn't stay here in Drygulch.

CHAPTER 5

Billy Joe was woken the next morning by feeling something wet against his cheek. He opened his eyes and found himself looking into the big brown eyes of the dog, Patch. As he watched the dog, it moved its muzzle forward and licked him on the face again.

'Yurk!' said Billy Joe, sitting bolt upright and pushing Patch away.

'He's only saying "Hello",' said Andy. 'Anyway, you're using his blanket.'

Billy Joe pushed himself to his feet and went to where his clothes had been drying by the stove. They felt warm and dry.

Patch sat down on the blanket and looked at Billy Joe as if to tell him 'This is *my* blanket.'

Billy Joe noticed there was a skillet on the top of the stove, with something cooking in it. Jess stood near it, poking it. It smelled good.

'What's that?' Billy Joe asked.

'Corn pancakes,' said Jess. 'You're gonna need something in your stomach before you head off.'

Jess pushed a knife beneath the pancakes and flipped them over to cook the other side. 'Breakfast in a few minutes, fellas,' he announced. 'Get the platters, Andy.'

Andy was obviously used to doing this, because he was already taking wooden platters from a box and bringing them to Jess. Billy Joe noticed there was a stack of pancakes that had been already cooked warming on the top of the stove.

Jess finished frying the pancakes in the skillet, then divided the whole lot on the wooden platters. Shane handed them out, one to each boy. As Billy Joe took his, he realized just how hungry he was, and how long ago it was since he'd eaten.

The pancakes were delicious, crispy and with a milky corn taste, with a few herbs thrown in to give them flavour.

'Do you do all your own cooking?' he asked.

'Depends,' said Jess. 'Me and Shane generally take turns. Pete tries, but he burns everything.'

'I can't be good at everything,' grumbled Pete, stuffing pancake into his mouth.

'Oh yeah?' chuckled Shane. 'And wh-wh-what exactly *are* you g-g-good at?'

Billy Joe tensed. That was the kind of insult that usually led to a fight. But, to his surprise, instead of leaping at Shane and attacking him, Pete laughed.

'Taking care of you, dogbreath,' Pete grinned.

'Pete's our handyman,' Jess told Billy Joe, chewing on his pancakes. 'He did most of the fixing up of this place.'

'It's because p-people take pity on h-him,' said Shane. 'They see he's so th-th-thin so they g-g-give him stuff like w-w-wood 'n' nails.'

'They don't give me stuff,' Pete corrected him firmly. 'I work for it. I do some work for Mr Brady at the timber yard and he gives me bits of wood left over. I work for Mr Schultz and he gives me nails he can't use. That's all.'

Billy Joe looked around the shack at the patching that had been done to make it sound from the rain.

'You've done a good job,' he said. 'Good as any grown-up carpenter.'

Pete said nothing, but Billy Joe could tell from the way he smiled that he'd said the right thing.

As the boys ate their pancakes, it struck Billy Joe with surprise that they all seemed relaxed with one another. They were like... Billy Joe struggled to find a word that described them. Brothers? That may be true of Pete and Shane. But what about Jess and Andy? Family, then? No, the nearest he could think of was the word 'tribe'.

Yes, these boys were a small tribe. And the tall boy, Jess, was their chief – their leader.

'When you've finished, it'd be a good idea to get you out of town early,' Jess suggested to Billy Joe. 'With luck, those cowboys will still be in bed, sleeping it off.'

'Yeah,' nodded Billy Joe. 'Early would be good.'

'W-w-where will you g-go?' asked Shane.

Billy Joe shrugged.

'I don't know,' he said. 'Whichever side of town I leave by, I'll start walking and just keep going till I come to another town.'

'The nearest town is Bluerock, about three days walk,' Jess told him. 'You'll need water and food.'

'Just water,' said Billy Joe. 'I got used to catching my own food, living out with my old man.'

'I kn-kn-knew he was an Indian!' said Shane.

'I ain't no Indian!' Billy Joe said angrily. 'My pa was a white man!'

'Calm down,' said Jess. 'Me, I'm mostly Scotch, part Cherokee, part Mexican, with a bit of French. That's what my pa told me before he died. The thing is, it don't matter where you come from. It's the kind of person you are that counts.'

Not if you look too much like an Indian, thought Billy Joe bitterly. Then he looked around the shack and the boys again and thought about what Jess had said. For all of these boys, it was about being a good person. Honest, even though they were poor. And they had all been hurt and rejected. That's what kept them together.

'The main thing is to get you out while it's safe,' continued Jess. 'I'll go with you as far as the town limits, to show you the way.' To the other boys, he asked, 'D'you know where you're all working today?'

'Me and Shane are gonna be at the livery stable,' said Pete. 'Shane's cleaning out the horses and there's some fences need fixing that I said I'd do.'

'I'm going to the saloon,' said little Andy proudly. 'Mr Prentice says he's got customers who want their boots shined.'

'Good,' nodded Jess. 'So, Pete, you take care of Shane and Andy and make sure they go to work.'

'W-w-we always go to w-w-work!' protested Shane indignantly.

'On time,' said Jess firmly.

'We're always on time,' said Pete, and there was a note of angry defiance in his voice as he said it. 'You don't need to keep on at us about that, Jess. We don't sneak off!'

'I never said you did!' protested Jess.

'Well you sure keep goin' on about it,' grumbled Pete. 'It makes me feel you don't trust us unless you're around to keep an eye on us.'

Jess sighed. 'OK, I'm sorry,' he said.

But Billy Joe could tell that Jess wasn't sorry. He may be everyone's friend, but he was also letting them know he set the rules and that the other boys had better live by them.

Billy Joe looked down at his clothes. They were still messy from the mud, but it had dried and would flake off as he walked. These clothes would do him until he found some more.

'Here,' said Jess. 'Take this.'

Billy Joe looked round, and saw that Jess was holding out a hat. He took it. It was a broad-brimmed Stetson, battered and worn, and at least a size too big.

Billy Joe took it and put it on, and it slipped down his head and came to rest on his ears.

'I can't hardly see,' he complained, taking it off.

'That's the point,' said Jess. 'If you can't see much, it'll hide your face good, just in case anyone's looking for you.'

Billy Joe put the Stetson on again and let it rest back on his ears.

'It's a good hat,' he said. 'Where'd you get it?'

'It was my pa's,' said Jess. He didn't add anything more, except to say, 'OK. Let's go.'

Billy Joe nodded goodbye to the other boys, then he and Jess set off for the road out of town.

As they left the shack, Jess whistled and Patch bounced up from the dirt floor and trotted after them. The two boys walked along, Billy Joe watching from beneath the brim of the hat, keeping an alert look-out for any sign of Boone, and Patch padded along, sniffing at the ground as they walked.

'He's trying to pretend he's a hunting dog,'

grinned Jess. 'The truth is, even though he's still a young dog, Patch went deaf in one ear ages ago, and his sense of smell ain't all it could be. I think whoever had him before didn't treat him right, which is how come he ended up running away and finding shelter in the shack. But he's a good dog. He likes to pretend everything's all right, and it seems to keep him happy.'

Billy Joe noticed that Jess was careful to stay away from the Main Street and keep to the back lanes. From what Billy Joe had seen of the town when he'd arrived with his pa, like many towns in the West, Drygulch consisted of one long, wide street, with boardwalk pavements running alongside both sides of the street. All the important buildings were on the Main Street: the bank, the saloon and hotel, the hardware store, the Sheriff's office and jail, the grocery store, the funeral parlour, dress shops, and every other kind of store. Further along, heading out of town, were the working buildings that needed more space, such as the blacksmith's forge and the livery stable. The Main Street was where people shopped and ate, sat on chairs on the boardwalk and talked and passed the time of day. Some of the shopkeepers lived in rooms over their stores, overlooking the wide dirt road, but most people lived in small houses in the narrower roads that backed onto it. All the buildings were made of timber nailed together.

About four narrow streets away from the Main Street was where the housing got poorer. Here, the houses were shacks, some of them looking like they were barely held together by nails and wood patches. There was little glass in the windows of these houses, just blinds that hung down to keep out the flies and other insects. It was among these houses that Jess and the boys had their shack. The good thing, from Billy Joe's point of view, was that it meant they didn't have to go anywhere near the Main Street and the saloon, where he expected Boone and his cowboys would still be. It also meant that Billy Joe and Jess didn't have far to walk to get to one of the four roads out of town.

'This is sure some middle-of-nowhere town,' commented Billy Joe sourly as they walked along the back lanes to the edge of town. When he'd arrived in the town with his pa, Billy Joe had seen Drygulch was surrounded by a vast plain in all directions. There was sandy desert turning to huge expanses of grassland to the south and east, with mountains and hills to the north and west.

'I don't know,' shrugged Jess. 'I quite like it. It's as good as most other.'

'You bin in lots of other towns?' asked Billy Joe.

'A few,' replied Jess. 'You?'

Billy Joe nodded.

'Too many,' he said. 'Me and my pa was always movin' around.'

'Why?' asked Jess.

Billy Joe was about to say 'Cos he was a gambler and a cheat and we was always being chased out,' but instead he shrugged and said, 'That's the way it was.'

Fortunately for Billy Joe, Jess didn't ask any more questions but instead started telling him about the town.

'Someone told me Drygulch came about because of it being a major stopping point on the great cattle drives,' explained Jess. 'They reckon the first building put up was a saloon to sell liquor to thirsty cowboys. Whatever the truth, since that first building went up it just sort of grew and it's kept growing.'

'How big is it?' asked Billy Joe.

'Maybe four hundred people in the town itself, with another few hundred living out on the ranches around,' said Jess. 'But when a cattle drive comes through, there could be another couple of hundred cowboys in town whooping it up.'

By the time Jess had finished talking, they had reached the dirt road that led out of town.

'This here's the main road,' said Jess. 'If you follow it, it'll take you to Bluerock, which is about fifteen miles away. It ain't as nice a town as Drygulch, but it's all right.'

Billy Joe was about to return the hat, shake Jess's hand and head on his way, when the other boy suddenly stopped and pulled Billy Joe back.

'Don't look,' he whispered warningly. 'Pretend you and me are just standing talking.'

'Why?' demanded Billy Joe. 'What's up?'

'There are men with rifles hiding out in rocks along the side of the road,' said Jess. 'And one of them looks like one of the men who was with that man, Boone, last night.'

'What?' exclaimed Billy Joe, alarmed. 'You mean they're watching out for me!'

'Maybe,' said Jess, worried. 'We'd better go back.'

He took hold of Billy Joe's arm and steered him back the way they'd come. Patch had hurried forward sniffing the ground, but Jess whistled, Patch stopped sniffing and bounced after them as they headed towards the town.

'Walk natural and slow,' he advised Billy Joe. 'Just like we're out for a stroll with nothing important to do.'

Although he tried to stroll along, as if nothing special was happening, Billy Joe felt fear rising in his chest, almost choking him. Boone's men were out there waiting for him!

CHAPTER
6

All the way back into town, Billy Joe found himself looking into the alleys and side streets for men with guns. What was going on? Why was Boone so desperate to get hold of him? Was it because he'd seen Boone shoot his father?

The two boys and Patch arrived back at the shack, just as the other boys were leaving.

'W-w-we're going to w-work!' protested Shane, thinking that Jess had come back to check up on them. Then he spotted Billy Joe. 'W-what's happened?' he asked.

'There are men guarding the Bluerock road out of town,' said Jess.

'What?' asked Pete. 'Why?'

'You th-think they're a-a-after him?' asked Shane, pointing at Billy Joe.

'I don't know,' said Jess thoughtfully. 'Pete, I want

you and Andy to take a stroll out on the road east. Shane, you take the west road. Me and Patch'll go to the road south.'

Billy Joe noticed that Pete seemed to bridle at Jess giving him orders, but he said nothing, just spat on the ground.

'What are we looking for?' he asked.

'We're trying to find out if all the roads in and out of town are covered,' explained Jess. 'If we find one that isn't, then that's the one Billy Joe leaves by.'

'What about me?' demanded Billy Joe. 'What should I do?'

'You stay here in the shack,' said Jess, 'just in case it *is* you they're watching out for.' To the other boys, he added, 'Don't take no risks, now. Just walk out as if you're going for a stroll. If you see anyone, or anyone stops you, just be polite and come back. These men could be dangerous.'

The boys nodded and hurried off on their mission. Billy Joe looked at Jess gravely.

'I don't know why they want me so bad,' said Billy Joe. 'I saw him shoot my pa, but they know I ain't gonna do anything about it!'

'Maybe Boone don't. Remember what he said about not leaving you alive to kill him,' Jess reminded him. He frowned. 'But it sure does seem a strange lot of effort and a whole lot of men just to catch you. It don't make sense. Anyhow, maybe we'll find something out.

You just stay here and wait. We'll be back.'

With that, Jess set off with Patch running around his feet.

Billy Joe watched them go, then he went back inside the shack. A deep sense of pain and tragedy hung over him, like a dead weight around his heart.

For the next hour Billy Joe sat in the shack, wondering what was going on outside. All the time his ears were alert for any sound at the door, worried in case Boone or his gunmen should suddenly burst in. When the door did open, it was Jess and Patch who came in first. They were followed shortly after by Pete and Andy, and finally by Shane.

'They got two men covering the east road out towards River Creek,' announced Pete.

'Just the same as you described the men on the Bluerock road. They were hiding behind rocks, with rifles,' added Andy.

'S-same with the road out to the w-west,' confirmed Shane.

'And I saw a couple watching the road to the south,' said Jess. 'Like before, I recognized them from last night. They were with Boone. He's definitely behind all this.'

'It seems like they got the whole town cut off,' murmured Pete.

Shane looked at Billy Joe with awe on his face.

'Th-they must want you awful bad!' he whispered.

Billy Joe's mind was in a whirl. Why were Boone and his gang doing all this just to catch one small boy?

'I don't reckon they're after Billy Joe at all,' said Jess grimly. 'I reckon they're after the gold shipment.'

The other boys looked at Jess, then one another, before Pete exclaimed, 'Of course! I forgot it was today!'

'What gold shipment?' asked Billy Joe.

'It comes through about once a month,' said Jess. 'It's a stagecoach loaded with chests of gold to pay the soldiers at Fort Apache. The stagecoach stops here at Drygulch to turn the gold into coins at the bank, and to change horses.'

'B-but the stage always c-c-comes with an escort of s-soldiers,' pointed out Shane.

'That's right,' nodded Jess. 'And Boone has got a whole army of men in town with him. If you ask me, they're lining up to ambush the stage when it arrives at the bank.'

'But why've they put men on all the other roads?' asked Andy.

Patch obviously picked up the tone of worry in Andy's voice and came to the small boy, who bent down and hugged the dog close.

'If Jess is right, then I reckon it's to make sure no one leaves town and gets a warning out,' said Pete thoughtfully.

Billy Joe looked at them, stunned.

'You mean they're not after me?' he said. A huge feeling of relief flooded through him, like a weight being lifted.

'I don't think so,' said Jess. 'But it still ain't good news. Right now you're trapped along with everyone else in this town. And if Boone sees you, he might still shoot you.'

At Jess's words, the weight came back down on Billy Joe. He was still caught.

'I think we gotta tell the Sheriff what's happening' said Pete firmly.

'Good thinking,' nodded Jess. He turned to Shane, 'You and Andy had better get to work. Me and Pete will go and talk to the Sheriff. Billy Joe, you stay here till we get back.'

'I'm coming with you,' Billy Joe told them firmly. 'Staying in this place alone gives me the creeps. And I ain't got no work to go to.'

'OK,' nodded Jess. 'Better take Patch along to the livery stable with you, Shane. I got a bad feeling about things and if things go wrong and those gunmen come looking for us, I don't want them just finding Patch here on his own. That dog ain't gonna be no match for a man with a gun, good watchdog or no.'

'W-will do,' said Shane. He grinned. 'I'll tell M-Mr P-Pedersen that P-Patch has c-come to do P-Pete's work for him instead.' Shane grinned. 'I b-betcha he thinks P-Patch is more use.'

Shane and Andy headed off, with Patch bouncing along beside them.

'All right,' said Jess. 'Let's go see the Sheriff.'

Once more Billy Joe found himself walking through the back alleys of the town until they came to the Main Street. All the while, he felt a sickness in his stomach, half-expecting a gunman to appear out of nowhere at any second and shoot him down. They reached the Main Street and suddenly Jess stopped.

'Back up!' he whispered urgently.

Billy Joe and Pete stepped back into the alley.

'What's going on?' asked Pete.

Jess joined them in the shadow by the side of the building and gestured with his thumb towards the Main Street.

'Two of Boone's men are sitting outside the Sheriff's office, with rifles resting on their laps.'

'Where's the Sheriff?' asked Pete.

'Maybe he's gone out of town?' suggested Billy Joe. 'Maybe he's found out what's happening and he's gone to get help?'

Jess shook his head.

'His horse is still there, tethered to the rail. My guess is he's either inside his own jail, or else...'

Jess didn't finish, just gave a deep sigh. Billy Joe

and Pete knew what Jess had left unsaid. The bandits might have killed Sheriff Nolan.

'How are we going to find out?' asked Pete.

Jess thought about it for a moment, then said, 'Only one thing to do. I'll go over to the Sheriff's office and keep those two men talking. You two see if you can sneak round the back to where the cell window is. Climb up and see if you can see what's going on.'

Pete looked doubtful. He gestured at Billy Joe.

'Say Boone's in there and he sees Billy Joe?' he asked. 'He'll shoot him sure as eggs is eggs.'

'I won't give him the chance. I can run away pretty fast,' said Billy Joe, surprising himself at the confidence with which he said those words.

'If you're sure,' said Jess, still doubtful.

Billy Joe nodded firmly.

'Sooner we find out what's going on, the better,' he said.

'OK,' said Jess. 'We'll meet up in the alley just along from the Sheriff's office. Let's go.'

CHAPTER 7

While Billy Joe and Pete hurried off along the alley, heading to the back of the Sheriff's office and the small jail, Jess stepped out onto the Main Street. He climbed onto the boardwalk and ambled slowly towards the main entrance to the Sheriff's office. As he stopped outside it, the two men sitting there exchanged looks, then picked up their rifles from their laps.

'Can we help you, son?' asked one of the men.

'I'm here to see the Sheriff,' said Jess, and he made for the door.

Immediately, the other man leapt to his feet and planted himself firmly in front of the door, using his rifle to block Jess's path. He scowled grimly at Jess, his expression made worse by a vicious-looking scar down one side of his face.

'No one's seeing the Sheriff,' he growled menacingly.

Jess stopped. The sight of the rifle in Scar's hand made his heart beat faster, but he did his best not to let his fear show.

'Why?' asked Jess, feigning innocence.

He studied the two men. Both of them wore dirt-stained clothes, showing they spent time on the road. Both had pistols in their belts, as well as the rifles they held. The man with the scar looked dangerous, but the other, who had a big black moustache, seemed calmer.

'Why do you want to see the Sheriff, son?' asked Moustache.

'See if he's got any errands for me,' said Jess. 'I usually call and see if he needs me to do anything.'

'What sort of errands?' demanded Scar harshly.

'Different things,' replied Jess. 'Sometimes he gets me to feed and water his horse. Sometimes I clean his spare pair of boots.'

Scar shook his head.

'Listen, kid, the Sheriff don't want no errands done today,' he said. 'So why don't you just get on your way.'

'OK,' said Jess.

He turned to go, then stopped, playing for time. If he could just get inside the jail . . .

'Is it all right if I see him?' he asked.

Scar scowled, and the scar down the side of his face became livid. He lifted the rifle so that the barrel pointed right at Jess's face.

'Maybe you ain't hearing so good, kid,' he snarled, and his eyes narrowed dangerously. 'The Sheriff don't want no errands run. He ain't seeing anyone today. Now get away from here before I decide to shoot some sense into that head of yours.'

'Hey now, Pat,' said Moustache, and he reached out and pushed down Scar's rifle. 'Ain't no need for that. He's just a kid.'

Scar spat on the boardwalk.

'He may be just a kid, but Boone give us our orders,' he said. 'No one gets in or out of the Sheriff's office without his say-so.'

Jess gave an apologetic shrug.

'I'm sorry, sir,' he said. 'I wasn't meaning no harm. But I'd be grateful if you tell the Sheriff I called. I don't want him thinking bad of me.'

'Don't you worry, son, we'll tell him that,' said Moustache, and he winked at Jess. 'Now you'd better run along.'

'Yes, sir,' said Jess.

The boy walked calmly back along the boardwalk and into the alley. Pete and Billy Joe were already there, waiting there for him. They both looked agitated.

'Jess, we got big trouble,' blurted out Pete.

'The Sheriff . . .' began Billy Joe.

Jess shook his head and put his finger to his lips to silence them.

'Let's get away from here and talk,' he said. 'Sound carries. The two guys at the front will hear us. Or someone else will.'

Billy Joe and Pete followed Jess down the alley away from the Main Street, and then along the back street until they came to the corral near the livery stable. The fenced-off area was empty. Jess took a careful look around to make sure they couldn't be overheard, then turned to Pete and Billy Joe.

'OK,' he said. 'Tell me what you learnt about the Sheriff.'

'We spoke to him,' said Pete. 'He was in the cell in his jail. I climbed up on Billy Joe's shoulders and talked to him through the window.'

'Is he all right?' asked Jess.

Pete nodded.

'He is at the moment. He says the bandits came into his office and took his guns off him and locked him in his cell. He guesses the same as you do, that it's something to do with the gold shipment that's coming in today. He reckons Boone has got about forty men in town. They must have come in last night.'

'How's he doin'?'

Pete shrugged.

'He looked OK. I guess he didn't even have a chance to fight back when they came in.'

'Does he know much about Boone?' asked Jess.

Again, Pete shrugged.

'He just said it was Boone who locked him up.'

'At least the Sheriff's still alive,' mused Jess. 'That's something. Was there anyone else inside the jail?'

'Not that I could see and the Sheriff didn't say.'

'So I guess most of Boone's men will be somewhere near the bank, staking it out,' said Jess thoughtfully.

'And inside it,' added Pete.

Jess nodded in agreement.

'What are we going to do?' asked Billy Joe.

'That depends,' said Jess. 'There ain't no one else but the Sheriff in charge here.'

'Isn't there a Deputy?' asked Billy Joe.

'Yeah, but he's away back east at the moment,' replied Jess.

'We gotta tell someone!' urged Pete. 'What about Mayor Redding?'

Jess laughed.

'Mayor Redding?' he chuckled. 'Come on, Pete! You know he's the most crooked man there is! What's he gonna do?'

'Well, maybe he can get a posse together,' suggested Pete.

Jess shook his head.

'I can't see it,' he said doubtfully. 'Mayor Redding is only interested in one thing. Making as much money as he can from his bank and from selling people licences.'

'But there ain't no one else,' Pete pointed out.

'Pete's right, Jess,' pressed Billy Joe. 'We gotta do something. Sheriff Nolan's a good man. You said so yourself.'

Jess stood and thought about it.

'Trouble is, I don't trust the Mayor.'

'Then what *do* we do?' asked Pete, a note of desperation in his voice.

'We gotta get past them and get outa town some way,' said Jess. 'So we can warn the stage before it gets here.'

'Not me!' said Billy Joe fervently. 'After what Boone said, I'll get shot for sure if they see me.'

'And they've got every road in and out of town covered,' Pete pointed out.

'I'll go along the dry creek that runs between the Bluerock and Creek roads,' said Jess. 'There's some gulleys there I might be able to get through without them seeing me.'

'I'll come with you,' said Pete.

Jess looked at Pete, shaking his head.

'No, Pete,' he said. 'Just in case things go wrong, you're going to be needed here to look after Shane and Andy.'

'Say you're caught?' asked Billy Joe.

'We've got no choice,' said Jess. 'I'll take Patch with me. If anyone sees us, I'll say we're going out hunting. They might believe me.'

'They might not,' said Pete.

'Like I said, it's a chance we gotta take,' said Jess.

'What about Shane and Andy?' asked Pete. 'We gonna tell them what's goin' on?'

'We'll tell Shane,' said Jess. 'With Andy, we don't want to say anything that scares him. You know what he's like, he'll go running round shouting and causing a panic.' He gave a concerned frown. 'Let's wait and see what happens to me and Patch first.'

CHAPTER 8

Jess, Pete and Billy Joe moved along to the livery stable at the edge of the Main Street. When they got there, Shane was clearing up horse manure with a pitchfork and piling it onto a wooden wheelbarrow. Patch lay in the sun, his tongue hanging out, panting slightly as he watched Shane work.

'W-what's the n-news?' asked Shane.

Briefly, Jess filled him in: Sheriff Nolan in jail, under guard.

As Jess talked, Pete looked along the almost empty street.

'Is it just me, or are there less people around than there usually are at this time of day?' he asked frowning.

The boys looked up and down the street. Pete was right. Normally at this time of day, the street would be full of people going about their business. Today there was no one around, except the armed men sitting outside the Sheriff's office, and old Mr Pantages, sitting outside the hardware store smoking a pipe as he always did.

'They know something's going on,' said Jess thoughtfully.

'Th-th-then w-why isn't anyone doing anything about it?' asked Shane.

Jess turned to Shane.

'What did Mr Pedersen say when you got to the livery stable this morning?' he asked.

'He j-just told me to collect up the horse manure and put it on the d-dung heap,' said Shane.

'Nothing else?'

'Nope,' Shane shook his head. Then he added, 'W-w-which is strange, because usually Mr P-Pedersen likes to talk. But today he just w-w-went back inside his house. Usually he's doing st-stuff with the horses, or ch-checking the leather.'

'We gotta do something,' muttered Pete, with a determined look in his eyes.

'And we will,' nodded Jess. He turned to Shane. 'I'm gonna see if I can sneak outta town and try and warn the stage. I'll take Patch with me so if I get caught I can say we're going huntin'.'

Shane looked at Patch and grinned.

'Th-that dog ain't never had so much exercise in a m-m-moon's age!' he chuckled. 'Two-two long walks in one d-day. He's sure g-g-gonna be sleeping g-good tonight!'

Jess whistled at Patch, and the dog got up and bounced over to him, tail wagging.

'Come on, Patch. We're going for another walk,' said Jess, then to Pete, he added, 'Take good care of everyone, Pete.'

'You can depend on it, Jess,' said Pete, his voice serious.

Jess nodded, then he and Patch walked off.

Pete turned to Billy Joe.

'OK, looks like I'm in charge for now,' he said. 'So, this is where you start to earn your food and keep, Billy Joe.' He pointed to the pitchfork stuck in the steaming pile of manure. 'Grab hold of that and let's all get working.'

Jess reached the rocky gulley at the edge of town that led down to the dried-up old river bed. Weeds and bushes gave good cover. He slid down the rocks and scrabbly scree to the dry river bed. He clicked his fingers and Patch scrambled down the rocks and dusty sides of the gulley to join him. So far so good. Jess reckoned he was about a mile from either of the two roads out of town. If he could keep his head down and move slow . . .

BANG! Peeoww!!

Jess felt the bullet before he heard the shot. There was an explosion on a large boulder beside him and splinters of rock flew up into his face, one of them tearing into the skin on his forehead. He threw himself down on the hard dry caked ground. Already, he could feel the blood getting sticky on his skin.

'Stand up where I can see you, or I'll start firing and kill you for sure!' barked a harsh voice.

Billy Joe emptied a wheelbarrow load of manure and straw onto the growing pile at the back of the livery stable, then wheeled the barrow back along the fence towards the stable. Pete was hard at work fixing a couple of broken fenceposts and Shane was sitting on a wooden box, having a rest from the work.

It seemed strange to Billy Joe that there was this deadly threat of robbery and murder hanging over them, yet here they were, working as if it was just a normal day. It seemed so . . . ordinary. Not that Billy Joe had ever really lived an ordinary life. Life with John Ford had been spent on the run, moving from town to town, from camp to camp, always looking for a sucker to cheat at cards, or a way to beg for money.

He knew this stretch was only temporary. As soon as he could, he'd be out of this town and on the road again. But when he did, maybe he'd look for a proper honest job. It felt good.

Except, would he ever get out with a gang of killers in charge? The odds against Billy Joe even staying alive long enough to lead a normal life seemed pretty heavy. Sucker's odds, his pa would have called them. Odds you can't win against.

Suddenly he was aware of Pete and Shane arriving to stand beside him.

'We can't leave it like this, Billy Joe,' Pete said. 'We can't leave it all to Jess.'

'And s-say s-something happens to J-Jess,' put in Shane. 'W-we're losing p-precious t-time.'

'What do you suggest we do?' asked Billy Joe.

'I think we ought to go see the Mayor,' said Pete. 'I know he don't like us, but with the Sheriff in jail, we gotta tell someone what's going on. And he *is* the Mayor.'

Billy Joe looked at Shane, who nodded in agreement.

'OK,' he said. 'You know these people. I don't.'

Pete gestured along the street towards the Sheriff's office, and the two armed men still sitting outside it.

'But we'll go in the back way to his bank,' he said. 'We don't want those guys outside the Sheriff's office seeing us. They're suspicious enough already. And I think it's a good idea if we stick together. Things are starting to get dangerous in this town.'

'Th-th-think we ought to tell Andy what's going on?' asked Shane.

'No,' said Pete. 'For the moment, I reckon he's safer where he is, cleaning shoes over at the saloon.'

'But say Jess comes back and we ain't here?' asked Billy Joe.

'Good thinkin',' nodded Pete. He turned to his brother and said, 'Shane, you stay here and wait for Jess. If he comes back, tell him where me and Billy Joe have gone.'

Then Pete and Billy Joe headed off the Main Street and along the back lane to the rear entrance of Redding's bank. As they reached it, they heard a harsh voice from inside Redding's office come to them from the half-open window.

'All we're looking for is a little common sense, Mr Mayor. We get that, and everything's gonna be fine,' said the voice.

Billy Joe recognized the voice at once, and a bolt of fear shot through him.

Boone!

Patch nuzzled Jess's face, licking at the blood and whining in concern. *If that gunman hears the dog*, thought Jess . . .

'I said stand up where I can see you!' shouted the voice again. 'With your hands in the air!'

Reluctantly, Jess got to his feet, wiping the blood

out of his eyes as he put his hands over his head. His forehead hurt where the rock splinters had hit him.

Patch began to bark, and Jess saw a cowboy approaching, the rifle in his hands pointed straight at Jess. The cowboy quickly switched the aim of the rifle towards Patch.

'If that dog makes a move for me, he's dead for certain,' warned the cowboy. 'Call him off!'

'Easy, Patch,' said Jess as he reached down towards the dog to get hold of him.

'Keep those hands where I can see them!' shouted the man. He was scrambling over rocks as he reached the dry river bed, heading towards Jess and Patch.

'I'm just taking hold of the dog so he don't rush at you,' said Jess.

'OK,' grunted the cowboy. 'One hand only, though. Keep your other hand up in the air.'

Jess grabbed the loose skin at the back of Patch's neck with one hand and held it. Patch was growling and Jess knew he was getting ready to jump at the man holding the gun.

'Easy, Patch. Easy,' said Jess gently.

The cowboy had clambered down into the dry creek now. He kept a safe distance from Jess and Patch, but kept his rifle aimed firmly at them.

'Where d'you think you're going?' he demanded.

'Hunting,' replied Jess. He gestured at Patch, who now stood panting beside him. 'Me and my dog.'

'Hunting what?' asked the man.

'Snakes and lizards,' said Jess. 'We skin 'em and sell 'em. The meat tastes good and their skins make real good coverings for boots and stuff. A guy back east . . .'

'Shut up!' barked the man. 'You ain't gonna be doing any hunting today.'

Jess frowned.

'Why?' he asked.

'Cos I said so,' snapped the man.

'But . . .' began Jess.

The man pointed the rifle firmly at Jess's face, and Jess felt his stomach turn to water. He stopped talking, and swallowed hard.

'Cos there's an illness in town,' said the man. 'We bin told not to let anyone in or out. Anyone who tries to go in or out gets shot. That's my orders.'

'OK,' said Jess hastily. 'I ain't goin' anywhere.'

'Good,' said the man.

Jess waited, but the cowboy didn't move.

'What illness?' asked Jess, pretending to be curious.

The cowboy frowned.

'What?' he said.

'This illness,' asked Jess. 'What sort of illness is it? I'm thinking it must be pretty dangerous if people ain't allowed to come in or leave town.'

The cowboy looked uncomfortable and Jess realized that Boone obviously hadn't prepared his men for questions.

'The reason I asked . . .' continued Jess.

'Shut up!' barked the cowboy again. He levelled the rifle even more firmly at Jess. 'No one knows what it is, which is why a doctor's been sent for. All I bin told is to shoot anyone who tries to go in or out. Now, you can either carry on walking out and get shot, or walk back into town.'

'No trouble, sir,' said Jess quickly. 'Me and my dog here, we're going back into town.' He smiled at the man. 'I sure hope that doctor gets here soon so we can find out what this illness is. I got some big orders for snakeskins.'

With that, Jess turned and began to scramble up the rocks and scree out of the dry creek, pulling Patch after him. All the time he was aware of the cowboy with the rifle watching him, and his own heart thumping like it was going to burst out of his chest with fear.

The bandits had the town surrounded. There was no way in or out.

CHAPTER 9

Pete and Billy Joe moved closer to the half-open window and crouched down below it, hiding behind a stack of boxes that had been left near the door.

'I'll say it again so we're both very clear on what's happening,' they heard Boone say. 'I've got men stationed all around this town. No one gets in or out without my say-so. We've got your Sheriff locked up safely in his own jail. My men are inside this bank and in the houses on the other side of the street.

'It's gonna be very simple. The stage and the military arrive, unload the gold and bring it into the bank. We take the gold, tie them up and ride off out of here.

'All we want is for everyone in this town to go around like normal. When we've done what we came to do, we'll leave. No one will get hurt.'

'What happens if the soldiers put up a fight?' came another voice, that of Mayor Redding.

Boone chuckled. 'That's not something you need to worry about, Mayor. If they're sensible, they'll just put their hands up. I understand there'll only be about ten men with the gold. I've got forty here with me. It don't make sense for them to put up a fight. But, whichever way, it ain't your problem. All you have to think about is that none of this is going to come back on you.'

'But we'll be held responsible,' insisted Redding. 'They'll know you were here and we didn't do anything.'

'Because you couldn't.' said Boone. 'Your Sheriff was in jail. We held you all hostage. So long as you remember that, everything will be all right.' Then he added, 'Of course, there will be some compensation for your trouble, providing no one proves difficult.'

'What sort of compensation?' asked Mayor, and there was no mistaking the tone of eager greed in the Mayor's voice.

'I'm sure there'll be enough gold in that shipment for some to go to someone in this town who might be . . . helpful,' said Boone. 'We offered it to the Sheriff, but I'm afraid he didn't see the sense of it.'

'Yes, he can be an awkward man,' agreed Redding.

Pete looked at Billy Joe and scowled as he heard this.

'All you have to do is remember our agreement,' Boone carried on. 'You keep spreading the word among the townsfolk that it's in their best interests to just keep out of our business and do nothing, and I'll see that you get a token of my appreciation.'

'Fine,' said Redding. Then he added, hastily, 'I'm only doing this for the safety of the town, of course. I'm just thinking of the people's best interests, like you said.'

'Of course,' agreed Boone.

The boys heard the sound of boots scuffling, and realized that Boone and the Mayor were heading towards the door. Quickly they pushed themselves even further behind the pile of boxes.

The door opened and Boone came out. There was a man with him, one of the men from the night before, when Boone had chased Billy Joe.

They shut the door behind them.

The other man looked at Boone quizzically.

'You really gonna give the Mayor a share of the loot?' he asked.

Boone laughed harshly. He shot a quick look towards the window of Redding's office, then lowered his voice.

'Am I?!' he grunted. 'When the ambush is over we're gonna kill everyone in this town. I don't want any witnesses left who can identify us. Everyone here is gonna die.'

Silently, Pete and Billy Joe waited until Boone and his henchman had gone, then they hurried back to the livery stable. They reached it at the same time as Jess and Patch appeared from the back roads of town. The boys were shocked to see the dried blood down the side of Jess's face.

'W-what happened?' asked Shane, staring at Jess.

'One of Boone's men shot at me,' said Jess. 'He missed. The bullet hit a rock.' He touched his forehead. 'Splinters did this.'

'You feelin' OK?' asked Billy Joe.

Jess shrugged.

'OK as I'll ever be,' he said. 'One thing's for sure, there's no way in or out of this town. Boone's men have got it sealed tight.'

Briefly he recounted what happened to him in the dry gulley.

'We got worse news than that,' said Pete grimly and he told Jess where they'd been. '. . . when the ambush is over and they've robbed the stage, they're gonna kill everyone in town.'

Jess stared at them in shock.

'You sure you heard right?' he asked.

'We heard Boone say it clear as anything,' nodded Billy Joe. 'They're gonna kill everyone. And that includes us.'

CHAPTER 10

'You m-mean we're gonna d-die?' gasped Shane, and he began to tremble with fear.

'Not if I can help it,' Jess said grimly. He took the younger boy by the shoulders and looked him determinedly in the face. 'Trust me, Shane. I ain't gonna let that happen.'

'So what are we gonna do?' asked Pete.

'M-maybe we c-could g-get help from outa t-town,' suggested Shane.

'How?' demanded Pete. 'Every road out is guarded. Like Jess just found, even the old creek is guarded!'

'The t-telegraph office,' said Shane. 'If we c-can get Mr P-Porter to s-send a w-wire to River Creek . . .'

'No chance!' snorted Pete. 'If Boone's got his men staking out the roads out of town, he's bound to have thought of the telegraph office. He'll have Mr Porter locked up.'

'Maybe, maybe not,' said Jess thoughtfully. 'I'm guessing Boone will want to keep the telegraph open in case anyone sends messages in. He won't want people outside to think there's anything wrong here at Drygulch.

'My guess is he'll have someone sitting with Mr Porter checking messages that come in and making sure that Mr Porter just sends back wires that don't stir things up.'

The boys thought about this.

'Maybe a couple of us ought to go to the telegraph office and see if Jess is right,' suggested Pete.

'M-me,' volunteered Shane.

'Why?' asked Billy Joe.

'B-because I g-go there a lot,' said Shane. 'I help Mr P-Porter. It's one of m-my jobs.' He smiled, pleased. 'And I know h-h-how the telegraph w-works . . . Mr P-Porter showed me. S-s-so even if Mr P-Porter can't send a m-message, I c-can do it.'

Jess looked at Shane, suspiciously.

'Are you sure, Shane?' he demanded. 'You ain't just boasting?'

'Honest!' insisted Shane. 'I asked Mr P-Porter how the telegraph w-w-w-worked, and he showed me. He showed me h-how to read 'em when they c-come in, and how to s-send 'em.'

Billy Joe looked at Shane with admiration.

'You can *read*?' he asked, impressed.

Shane nodded. 'I can read s-some. Telegrams and some of the B-Bible when the P-Preacher showed me. Can't I, Pete?'

Pete nodded in confirmation.

'Shane does some reading real good,' he said. 'Like he said, he read me some bits out of the Bible. And some newspaper stories as well. Cutting out some of the longer words.'

'And I'm l-learning the l-longer words,' said Shane. 'Mr P-Porter helps me. He shows me p-pieces from the paper, and the w-w-words in the telegraph instruction book.'

'But you sure you know how to send a wire?' insisted Jess. 'Which keys you tap, and the buttons you press, all that sort of thing?'

'I do!' nodded Shane. 'Mr P-Porter showed me!'

'And you know the codes for the different places?'

Again, Shane nodded.

'Yup!' he said. 'I know Bluerock and River Cr-Creek and Stackpole . . .'

'This might work,' said Jess.

'What might?' demanded Billy Joe. 'You thinking of him going in and sending a message?'

'Only if Mr Porter can't do it,' said Jess.

'You're mad!' exclaimed Billy Joe. 'The telegraph office is gonna be guarded as heavy as the roads!'

'It's a chance we'll have to take,' said Jess. 'The thing is, it's our only way. So we gotta try it.'

'It won't work,' said Billy Joe. 'Even if we get a message through to River Creek, how do we know it'll get to the stage or the army in time?'

'Billy Joe's got a point,' said Pete. 'That gold shipment will already be on its way. It'll already have left River Creek.'

'A fast rider might catch them up,' said Jess.

'*Might*,' stressed Pete.

'What else can we do?' asked Jess. 'You got any better idea, let's have it.'

Pete struggled, doing his best to come up with something else. Finally, he gave a deep sigh and shrugged.

'Nope,' he said. 'You're right, Jess.'

'And the qu-quicker we do it, the b-better!' said Shane.

'OK,' said Jess. 'Billy Joe, you, me and Shane will go to the telegraph office. Pete, you go to the saloon and pick up Andy. I reckon it's time to get him somewhere safe.'

'Why me?' demanded Pete. 'Why can't I go to the telegraph office?'

'Because somebody's got to make sure Andy is safely home and off the street,' stressed Jess. 'Now we know what's happening, we've all got to stick together as best we can. Billy Joe can't go into that saloon and get Andy, not after his old man being killed there last night. Boone or one of his men might be in there and see him. It can't be Shane because he knows how to work the telegraph. So it's got to be you.'

Pete shook his head.

'No,' he said, angrily. 'I always get the safe jobs. Like staying here and mending fences while you go out and get yourself shot.'

'It was in case . . .'

'I know what it was in case of!' snapped Pete. 'It's cos you don't think I can do anything!'

Jess stared at the angry Pete in surprise.

'That ain't so at all, Pete!' he protested.

'No?' demanded Pete. 'I'm the oldest after you, but you never let me do anything important! Yeah, I go to work, but so does Andy and he's only six years old.' Pete shook his head, and the boys could see the unhappiness on his face. 'I don't want to be the leader, Jess. That's you. It always has been and it always will be. But just for once I want to *do* something, not just follow. And especially in *this* case. Shane's my brother and I need to look after him! Let me do this!'

Jess hesitated, then he nodded.

'OK, Pete,' he said. 'You're right. You, Shane and Billy Joe go to the telegraph office. Size up what's happening there and see if you can get the chance for Mr Porter to send a message. Or, for Shane to do it.'

Pete beamed a broad smile of delight.

'Trust me, Jess!' he said happily.

Jess nodded, but the look on his face showed he didn't look happy himself. He turned to Shane and Billy Joe.

'Now you two listen to me,' he said to them firmly. 'You two gotta listen to Pete. What he says goes. Right?'

'Right,' nodded Shane.

Billy Joe hesitated. He wasn't used to taking orders from anyone except his pa. But the look on Jess's face showed he was deadly serious.

'Yeah, me too,' said Billy Joe.

'Right,' said Jess. 'I'll pick up Andy and see you back at the shack.' He was about to go, then he stopped and added heavily, 'And take real good care. These guys are killers.'

CHAPTER 11

The telegraph office was a wooden hut about a mile from the edge of town, on the south side. When the telegraph company had put in the posts and overhead wires a few years before, they had by-passed Drygulch. No one quite knew why. Either someone had read the map wrong, or someone didn't pay the right amount of bribe to the men putting in the posts. Whatever the reason, the result was that Drygulch ended up a mile away from the telegraph line.

Following complaints (and payments) the telegraph company agreed to open an office at Drygulch, but it would have cost too much money to divert the actual telegraph wire into the town. So a wooden hut was built next to the telegraph pole nearest to the town, one mile outside of it. The hut wasn't even on a road. A single track led to it from the town, and stopped.

Most visitors to Drygulch didn't even know the

telegraph hut was there because it was hidden in a small gulley flanked by rocky outcrops and some scrubby bushes.

Pete, Billy Joe and Shane were hiding behind these same bushes and rocks now, studying the hut.

There was one horse tethered outside the hut. They knew it didn't belong to Mr Porter, the telegraph operator, because Mr Porter didn't own a horse. He walked to the hut every day from the town, and walked back again.

The boys worked their way forward between the bushes and rocks so they could get a better view of the inside of the hut through the open door.

Mr Porter was sitting at the desk with the telegraph equipment on it. A gunman sat near him, a pistol in his hand.

'OK, so there's just the one of them here,' murmured Pete. 'All we gotta do is get him outside.'

'How?' asked Billy Joe.

'W-why don't we d-do the fire t-trick?' suggested Shane.

'What fire trick?' asked Billy Joe.

'It was a trick me and Shane played on Old Man Parsons,' explained Pete. 'We told him there was a fire in his outhouse. While he ran out to look, we snuck in and put a chicken in his kitchen. A real live chicken.' He chuckled. 'That chicken sure made some havoc! It was so funny!'

'J-Jess d-didn't think so,' said Shane. 'N-nor did Sheriff N-Nolan. He said he w-was g-gonna lock us up in the j-jail for d-disturbing the p-peace.'

'That was just what Jess got him to say to scare us,' said Pete. 'Anyway, I reckon the fire trick's as good as any. Billy Joe, you up to goin' in there and sayin' there's a fire at the back of the hut?'

Billy Joe nodded. If it meant a chance of stopping them all from being killed, he'd try anything.

'Yup,' he said. 'I can do that.'

'OK,' said Pete. 'Now if he leaves Mr Porter in there on his own, we're all right. But if he don't, Shane here will go in and do what he can about sending a message. That right, Shane?'

Shane nodded.

'Me, I'll stay here and keep watch,' said Pete. 'If I see anyone coming I'll raise a warning.'

'G-got it,' said Shane.

'OK, Billy Joe,' said Pete. 'It's up to you.'

Samuel Porter sat at his desk looking at the telegraph machine. His fingers itched to reach out and tap out a warning message, sending it down the line to River Creek so that the stagecoach with the gold would keep away from Drygulch. But one look at the hard-eyed gunman sitting in the chair at the side of the room, a six-gun in his hand, his stare fixed on Porter stopped the telegraph operator from trying it.

The gunman must have read Porter's thoughts, because he growled, 'I hope you ain't thinking of doin' anything stupid with that machine. Like sendin' a message.'

'No sir,' said Porter hastily.

'Make sure you don't,' said the gunman. 'You just do like Boone told you. Any messages come in, you read 'em out to me so I know what they say. If any of 'em want a reply, I'll tell you which ones you can reply to. But generally, you don't send out no messages at all until our business here is done. And if you try, I got orders to shoot you.'

'Yes, sir, you told me,' nodded Porter nervously.

'And now I'm telling you again, just in case you've forgotten,' said the gunman.

The sound of running footsteps from outside brought the gunman out of his chair, his six-gun levelled at the open door. Billy Joe ran in and skidded to a halt when he saw the gun pointing at him.

'What's the matter?' asked Porter. He frowned, puzzled. 'Who are you, kid?'

'Fire!' Billy Joe blurted out, an expression of panic on his face.

'What?!' Porter said in alarm, leaping out of his chair at once.

'Sit down!' snapped the gunman, jerking his gun at

Porter, who immediately sat down. Turning back to Billy Joe, he asked suspiciously, 'Where is this fire?'

Billy Joe pointed outside.

'It's a barrel at the back of the telegraph office,' he said.

The gunman sniffed, then shook his head dismissively.

'I can't smell nothin',' he growled.

'There's smoke at the moment,' insisted Billy Joe, 'but I saw flames comin' from it! It looks like it's gonna set fire to the hut!'

'OK,' snapped the gunman. To Porter, 'You step out there ahead of me so I can keep an eye on you! And keep your hands in the air where I can see 'em!'

Porter got out of his chair, put his hands up and walked out through the door.

'Now you!' said the gunman, jerking his pistol at Billy Joe.

Billy Joe followed Porter, with the gunman close behind him.

Outside, Shane and Pete saw the three leave the hut and head for the back of it.

'Now!' hissed Pete, as soon as the group disappeared round the corner.

Shane leapt out from his hiding place and ran to the open door of the telegraph hut. He ran to the desk and sat down at it. All the time his mind was frantically working, doing his best to remember what Mr Porter had told him about how to send a wire. He touched the keys. What was the code for River Creek?

Shane started sweating and he could feel his heart thumping. He'd proudly boasted to the other boys that he knew how to send a telegram. The truth was, he'd watched Mr Porter do it, and Mr Porter had allowed him to send a wire just the once, so Shane was sure he could do it. But now, faced with the keys and the machine, suddenly his memory of the time he'd sent the wire was going all fuzzy.

The codes! What was the code for River Creek? He began to remember numbers and letters, but that was just for Bluerock. What was River Creek?

✳ ✳ ✳

Outside, the gunman looked at the barrel and sniffed.

'There ain't no fire!' he snarled angrily at Billy Joe.

Billy Joe did his best to put on his innocent expression.

'There was!' he said. 'I saw smoke and flames!'

'Well there ain't no smoke and flames now!' Suddenly his eyes narrowed. 'Hey, ain't you the kid who's daddy got shot last night at the saloon.'

A bolt of fear shot through Billy Joe.

'No!' he said. 'My daddy's far away, back east.' He looked at the man, willing him to forget. But the man just peered closer.

'You sure look familiar,' the man said.

'No,' protested Billy Joe, shaking his head. 'I ain't from round these parts.'

'Then what are you doing comin' all the way out here?' demanded the man.

'I…I…' stammered Billy Joe. 'I come to send a wire.'

'Who for?' demanded the man.

'For . . . for the undertaker,' Billy Joe improvised. 'He wants to know where are the brass handles he ordered. He's got an urgent order for some coffins.'

'There ain't no wires goin' out today,' snapped the man. 'Now, get going, and stop wasting my time.'

'But . . .' began Billy Joe.

'I said git goin'!' snarled the man, and he pointed his pistol at Billy Joe.

Billy Joe gulped.

'Don't worry, I'm goin',' he said. 'I'm sure sorry to be wastin' your time.'

As Billy Joe backed away, he felt guilty. He knew he hadn't given Shane enough time. He'd given in too quickly. He should have kept the man talking. Argued with him. Anything to give Shane time to send the wire. But the cold killer expression in the man's eyes when he looked at Billy Joe had sent a sick feeling of fear deep into Billy Joe's stomach. He'd been alarmed, sure that the man was going to kill him. And he'd backed off too soon.

As he walked away, there was a turmoil of conflicting

emotions inside him. One side of him was desperate to get away from the man and stay alive. The other side wanted to run back, grab the man, and try again. Keep Shane safe. But he didn't. Billy Joe walked on, doing his best not to break into a frantic run, still feeling sick with fear.

The man watched Billy Joe as the boy headed towards the narrow track that went to the town, and then he jerked his pistol at Porter.

'You. Back to the office,' he grunted.

Porter nodded and went round the building and headed towards the open door. As he did so, he heard sounds inside. Suddenly it hit him that the boys were up to something . . . something to do with beating the gunmen. He stopped and turned.

'I think we ought to take another look at that barrel,' he said. 'Sometimes these things just smoulder for ages and suddenly they just burst into flames.'

But the man had heard the sounds, too, because he pushed Porter to one side and ran in through the open door.

Shane was sitting at the desk, his hand poised over the telegraph equipment.

'What in tarnation are you doing?!' exploded the man angrily.

Shane stared at the man, shocked, his mouth open.

'I asked you a question!' snapped the cowboy, and he levelled the gun at Shane.

Suddenly there was the clatter of running feet from outside and Pete burst in, hurling himself at the armed man, hitting him in the back.

The man stumbled forward a pace, then whirled round and fired, just as Pete threw himself at him again.

The bullet took Pete high in the face, just above his eyes, blowing out the back of his skull.

CHAPTER 12

Porter gave a moan as Pete's body crashed to the floor. He stared down at the dead boy, at the blood oozing from Pete's head.

'Why did you do that?' he asked, shocked. 'He meant no harm!'

'Shut up!' snarled the man.

He swung round towards the desk, but the seat behind it was empty.

'Where's that boy?' demanded the gunman.

He bent down to look under the desk. As he did so, Shane, who had taken cover behind it, made a run for the door.

The man spun round and let fly with a shot. The bullet just missed the running Shane and ripped a piece of wood out of the door frame.

The man ran to the door in pursuit, but Shane had made it to the rocks and he dived behind them.

'Come on out, boy!' yelled the man. He fired off another shot. 'Come on out with your hands up! Don't make me come looking for you!'

Behind the rocks, Shane cowered, shaking with fear and shock at what had just happened. He could see again Pete falling backwards, mess flying out from the back of his brother's head.

'Come on, out!' the man yelled again.

Shane crouched and shivered, rocking backwards and forwards, moaning silently to himself, biting hard on his lips to stop any actual sounds coming out. He heard the man snap 'Get behind that desk, you!' and knew that he had turned his attention back to Mr Porter.

Shane forced himself to peer carefully out from his hiding place.

The man was standing in the doorway, gun in hand, looking to left and right, listening for any sound that would show where Shane was. Then he must have lost patience because he turned towards the inside of the hut and walked in.

Shane took the moment to slip out from his hiding place and crawl through the brush and scrub of the gulley, moving slowly, one inch at a time so as not to make a sound. Finally, he reached the edge of the gulley. He felt sick. He struggled not to vomit as he climbed up the side of the gulley, looking back over his shoulder. The man had decided to stay inside the telegraph hut with Mr Porter, making sure that the operator didn't get the chance to send a message out.

* * *

Billy Joe sat hidden among the huge rocks that edged the single track to the telegraph hut, looking along the dusty path. Where were Shane and Pete? They should have been here by now.

He'd heard the shots. Had one of the boys been killed? If so, where was the other one? Or had they both been shot? Maybe the gunman had just shot the telegraph operator. In which case, where were Shane and Pete? Although there had been three shots . . .

Billy Joe wondered how long he should stay there before heading back to town and Jess.

'I should have kept him talking longer!' he told himself angrily. 'Whatever's happened is my fault!'

Suddenly he saw a movement at the side of the track. It was Shane, crawling along the edge of the track, keeping to what little cover there was.

Billy Joe shot a look at the telegraph hut. There was no sign of movement, the armed man was obviously inside the hut.

Billy Joe edged out onto the track and called 'Shane!' in a loud whisper.

Shane hesitated, then got up and ran towards Billy Joe, crouching low as he did so. As Shane got near,

Billy Joe could see that Shane was crying, the tears running down his face leaving streaked marks in the dirt on his skin. Shane reached Billy Joe, and fell to his knees, sobbing.

'P-Pete's dead!' he moaned. 'He sh-shot Pete!'

Billy Joe gaped, stunned.

'Pete?' he said, his head in a whirl.

Shane nodded, still crying and trembling.

'He b-blew his head off right in f-front of me!'

'We got to get back to town and tell Jess!' said Billy Joe urgently.

Shane stayed where he was, kneeling on the dusty ground, his head bowed, sobbing and muttering Pete's name over and over again.

'Come on, Shane!' urged Billy Joe. 'If he comes looking for us he'll kill us just like he did Pete! Come on, Shane!'

'He w-was my b-b-big b-brother!' sobbed Shane, his grief making his stammer worse. 'He al-always l-looked out for me! And n-n-now he's dead. B-because of me!'

'No!' whispered Billy Joe fiercely. 'It wasn't your fault, Shane!'

Inside his head, Billy Joe once again told himself bitterly: *It was my fault. I let the gunman go too soon.*

Shane was lying on the ground, now, sobbing uncontrollably, his hands over his face, his body shaking with crying. Billy Joe reached down and grabbed him.

'We have to get back to the shack!' he said urgently. 'We have to tell Jess what's happened! Come on, sit up! Get up!'

Shane struggled to sit up. His face was streaked with tears and dirt.

'It w-was my f-fault!' he said. 'If I hadn't s-said I could send a w-wire . . .'

'Did you send it?' asked Billy Joe.

Shane shook his head miserably.

'I got scared! W-when I sat d-down at the machine I got all c-confused. I couldn't even remember the codes! Then, w-when I did I j-just s-sent the c-call sign and that m-man came back in before I could even s-start sending the m-message!'

Shane began to cry again.

'Pete's dead and it's my fault!' he moaned.

'Maybe River Creek will send a message asking what the rest of the message was?' suggested Billy Joe. 'Then the telegraph operator might be able to send an answer.'

Shane shook his head.

'The g-guy who killed Pete will make sure he d-don't,' he said.

'He still might,' insisted Billy Joe. 'We gotta hope! And right now, we gotta get back and tell Jess what happened. Come on Shane! You gotta get up! We gotta deal with this! Pete wouldn't want you to stay here and get killed as well!'

Slowly, Shane nodded. He was still crying, but doing his best to get it under control.

'Come on!' urged Billy Joe. He grabbed Shane under the arms and lifted him up until he was on his feet.

'Right, let's go!'

CHAPTER 13

Andy sat in the doorway of the shack with Jess and Patch. He lay with his head on Patch's body. Patch liked Andy doing this. Andy liked it too. The dog was warm. OK, so he had fleas, but so did most everyone. Fleas weren't as bad as the big horse flies that hung around the livery stable and wherever there were horses and cattle. Those were big insects that really hurt when they bit.

Andy saw Jess looking up and down the road.

'They bin gone a long time, Jess,' he said. 'Think they're all right?'

Jess nodded his head.

'They'll be OK, Andy,' he said. 'They're on a mission, and it ain't straightforward, so it's gonna take 'em more time than usual.'

Despite the confidence of his tone, Jess was worried. The boys should have been back by now.

He'd managed to get Andy out of the saloon without any awkward questions being asked, mainly because there hadn't been many people inside it. Just the bar-keep and some of the dancing girls. And a couple of Boone's men who barely even looked up from their card game. Everybody else was obviously staying at home where they would be safe.

A few simple questions to the bar-keep had established that Andy hadn't said anything about the robbery while he'd been in the saloon. Mostly he'd talked about Patch and what a clever dog he was. Jess had thought that was lucky. You never knew when Andy was going to do or say something that would land them all in trouble.

Something had gone wrong at the telegraph hut, he could feel it in his bones. Had Mr Porter or Shane managed to send the wire? Had they been caught?

Jess cursed himself silently.

I should have gone, he thought. *I should have been the one to take the risk.*

The sound of running feet on the road made him jerk round. Billy Joe and Shane were hurrying towards the shack. Even from this distance Jess could see that something was wrong. Shane was hunched over, holding himself. Was he hurt? Where was Pete?

'Stay here with Patch,' Jess ordered Andy, before he got up and ran towards the two oncoming boys. As he neared them he saw that Shane was crying.

'Pete's dead,' said Billy Joe. 'He got shot.'

Jess stared at them. He felt like a lead weight had hit his stomach.

Pete dead!

'How?' he asked, stunned.

'I w-was st-starting to s-send the w-wire when the man came in and c-caught me,' said Shane. 'He was g-gonna shoot me, and P-Pete ran in and j-jumped on him, and the man sh-shot him d-dead.' His face crumpled and he began to cry again.

'Pete's dead?' said a small shocked voice beside them.

It was Andy.

'I told you to stay with Patch!' said Jess angrily.

Andy began to cry, a low moaning sound.

'We've got to get off the street,' said Jess. He took Andy by the hand, and laid his hand on Shane's shoulder. 'Come on!' he said urgently, and he led them towards the shack.

It took time for the shock to sink in and for the boys to realize that Pete really was dead.

Shane sat crouched in one corner of the shack, his head down on his folded arms, while Andy cuddled into him. Both boys had stopped crying now, but their misery hung over both of them. Patch had woken up, aware that something bad had happened, and he moved from boy to boy, nudging each with his head, before finally settling with Andy, nuzzling the small boy with his wet nose to comfort him.

Jess and Billy Joe had moved apart from the others and conferred on the other side of the shack, watching the smaller boys as they did so.

Jess felt sick. Of all the gang, Pete had been his best friend. He felt guilty. If he'd argued more strongly with Pete . . . insisted he stayed . . . that he, Jess, had gone instead, like he'd originally said . . . then Pete would still be alive.

But this was no time for grief. Jess knew that the safety of the other boys depended on him staying strong.

'Shane's gotta stay here for the moment,' said Jess. 'Seeing Pete killed like that, he ain't gonna be no use for anything right now.'

He sank into silence, thinking hard.

'We gotta tell someone,' he said.

'Who?' demanded Billy Joe. 'The Sheriff's in jail. The Mayor's in on the robbery. They got the whole town sewn up tight.'

'I don't know,' admitted Jess. He thought for a moment, then said, 'We'll tell Mr Schmidt.'

'Who?' asked Billy Joe.

'He's the blacksmith.'

'What can he do?'

'I don't know,' admitted Jess. 'But he's big and tough. And he's honest. He don't like the Mayor neither.'

'One man on his own won't be able to do anything against Boone and his gunmen,' Billy Joe pointed out.

'No, but he might be able to make the Mayor listen to the truth about what's really going to happen after the robbery,' said Jess. 'The Mayor won't give us the time of day, but he'll have to listen to Mr Schmidt.'

'And what do you think will happen then?'

'Maybe the Mayor will get the townsfolk to fight back,' said Jess.

Billy Joe laughed scornfully.

'Not a chance!' he said. 'Me and Pete heard him talking to Boone. And you've already said the kind of man he is. A coward and a crook.'

'What other choice do we have?' Jess appealed to him. 'If nothing happens, we're all gonna die.'

Billy Joe thought it over, and nodded in glum agreement.

'When you say it like that, I guess you're right. We don't have no choice.'

Jess walked over to where Shane and Andy sat slumped.

'Me and Billy Joe are gonna go and see Mr Schmidt,' he told them. 'See if we can't get him to do something. Shane, you stay here and look after Andy. Don't take any risks. We'll be back as soon as we can.'

Shane nodded dully. He looked numb, still in a state of shock. Jess hesitated, as if he was going to say more, then decided against it. He turned to Billy Joe.

'Come on,' he said. 'Let's go see Mr Schmidt.'

CHAPTER 14

As Jess and Billy Joe walked along the Main Street towards the forge, they were aware the whole time of the two gunmen still sitting outside the Sheriff's office, rifles across their laps, and others of Boone's men dotted around the town. The two gunmen, Moustache and Scar, now had deputies' badges on, so they wouldn't look suspicious when the stagecoach and the army escort rode into town.

As Jess and Billy Joe passed the bank, they were aware of faces peering round the window from inside. The same was true of the houses and shops opposite the bank. Boone's men were stationed inside them, waiting for the order to come out shooting. Jess and Billy Joe forced themselves to walk along as slow and casual as they could, as they didn't want to startle any of the gunmen. Billy Joe was glad he was still wearing Jess's hat, which hid most of his face.

When they reached the forge, Schmidt, the big muscular blacksmith, was hard at work shaping horseshoes, taking the twisted metal out of the burning brazier of hot coals and hammering them into shape on his anvil. He stopped when he saw the two boys appear in the entrance to his forge.

'Jess,' he said. He chuckled, a rich fruity laugh. 'Seems to me you're late for work today. That ain't like you.' He looked at Billy Joe and asked, curious, 'Who's this?'

'This here's Billy Joe,' said Jess. 'He's new in town.'

The big blacksmith glared towards the men sitting outside the Sheriff's office and spat.

'Seems like there's lots of folks that are new in town,' he said grimly.

Jess nodded, then blurted out.

'Mr Schmidt, there's gonna be a robbery!'

The big man looked at them, before he nodded ruefully.

'I know,' he said with a heavy sigh. 'The Mayor's already come and seen me and told me. He says they got the Sheriff locked up in his own jail.'

'Yes, sir, they have,' said Jess.

Schmidt shook his head. He was obviously very angry and at the same time very frustrated.

'It makes me sick,' he growled. 'Trouble is, what can I do? If I had my way, we'd run them fellers outa town. But I'm just one man and the Mayor says there's forty of them, all born killers. With the Sheriff locked up as he is, what chance has one man got against that gang?'

'People are gonna get killed,' said Jess seriously.

Schmidt shook his head. 'The Mayor says nothing's gonna happen to anyone here providin' we just keep our heads down and let them do what they come here to do.'

'The Mayor's lying!' burst out Billy Joe.

Schmidt scowled.

'That don't surprise me none,' he said. 'I always knowed he was a lying buzzard, which is why I never voted for him to be Mayor.'

Jess shook his head sadly.

'He ain't lying,' he said. 'It's just that he ain't been told the truth by the leader of this gang. Billy Joe heard Boone tell his men that once the robbery is over, they're gonna kill everyone in this town to make sure no one says anything against them.'

The blacksmith looked sharply from Jess to Billy Joe, then back again at Jess.

'You sure of this?' he demanded.

'I ain't never lied to you, Mr Schmidt, and I ain't startin' now,' said Jess. 'Billy Joe here heard the man Boone say it, sure as night follows day.' He looked down, then he added in a quiet voice, 'They shot Pete.'

Schmidt stared at Jess.

'Pete?' he asked, his voice hollow.

The two boys nodded.

'Shot him dead,' added Billy Joe.

'Where?'

'Out at the telegraph office. Shane and Pete and Billy Joe went out there to try and send a wire to River Creek to warn them.'

'There was one man holding the telegraph operator prisoner,' continued Billy Joe. 'He caught Shane trying to send a message, and Pete ran in to save Shane. The man killed him. Blew Pete's head off, Shane said.'

The big blacksmith's fist tightened around the handle of his hammer and his face grew tight with silent fury.

'Those murdering cowards!' he breathed.

He put down his hammer and headed determinedly out into the Main Street, a look of anger on his face.

Billy Joe and Jess threw concerned looks at one another, then hurried after him.

'Where are you going, Mr Schmidt?' asked Jess.

'I'm going to see the Mayor,' replied Schmidt.

'Do you think he'll believe us?' said Jess.

'He'll believe me,' said Schmidt grimly.

'You better be careful,' Billy Joe warned him. 'They'll kill you as soon as look at you if they think you're making trouble.'

'Don't worry, I'll be careful,' Schmidt assured them. He stopped and turned to the boys, 'What happened to Pete's body?'

Jess looked at Billy Joe, who shrugged.

'I guess it's still out at the telegraph office hut,' he said. 'There was only one man there, and I guess he can't leave the hut to get rid of a body.'

The blacksmith nodded.

'You boys go back to the forge and wait,' he said.

'To be honest, it ain't really safe for us to be waiting anywhere, Mr Schmidt,' said Jess apologetically. 'We'll stay in Drygulch for sure, but we're gonna keep moving to stay safe.'

Schmidt nodded again.

'Makes sense,' he said. 'But stay in touch. We're gonna get this sorted this out.'

With that, the big blacksmith continued on his way towards the bank. The boys watched him go.

'We gonna wait for him?' asked Billy Joe.

Jess shook his head.

'Best thing we can do is keep out of the way,' he said. 'Once Mr Schmidt tells the Mayor about what we've said, it wouldn't surprise me if he tells Boone. And if he does that, you can bet Boone'll come lookin' for us. Which means we got to find a place for us all to hide.'

CHAPTER 15

Mayor Redding sat at his desk, tapping his fingers rapidly on the dark wood of the desktop. The Mayor was frightened. He'd met bad characters before, but there was something about this Boone that sent a chill of fear through him.

OK, there had been the offer of money. With any other crook, the Mayor might have haggled. But one look into Boone's eyes and Redding knew this was not a man it paid to annoy. Boone would kill Redding and anyone else as soon as look at them. The important thing was to make sure everyone in Drygulch came out of this alive and safe. Yes, there was a chance there'd be casualties. The army escort. The stagecoach driver. But only if they resisted. Providing they saw sense and just handed the shipment over, everything would be fine. No one would get hurt. And Redding was sure the army escort would hand the money over.

The escort usually numbered just ten soldiers. Boone had twice that number in the bank alone, all heavily armed with pistols and rifles. There were at least another fifteen of Boone's men in the shops and houses opposite, plus about another few watching the other roads in and out of town. Surely there was no way the soldiers would try and take on that many gunmen.

The Mayor looked at the clock. Ten o'clock. The shipment was due in just after noon. Two hours or so, and this would be all over and they could all go back to their business. Not that there was any business going on at the bank today. He'd sent the bank tellers home on Boone's instructions and word had spread for everyone to avoid going near the bank today. Everyone except the owner of the bank, Mayor Redding. Boone had been insistent that Redding stay right where he was and keep an eye on things.

So all Redding could do was sit, wait, worry and hope that Boone had his trigger-happy gunmen under control. There'd already been one man shot dead by the gang. Some gambler who'd been caught cheating.

Suddenly the door of his office burst open, and Redding leapt to his feet in alarm, terrified it might be one of Boone's gunmen. But it was just the blacksmith, Otto Schmidt.

Redding scowled and did his best to recover his dignity.

'Really, Mr Schmidt!' he snapped, annoyed. 'Do you normally enter a man's private office without knocking?'

'Those gunmen have killed Pete!' growled Schmidt.

Redding stared at the blacksmith, bewildered.

'Pete?' he repeated, puzzled, not sure who the blacksmith was talking about.

'One of Jess's boys,' said Schmidt.

Suddenly Redding realized. Schmidt meant the gang of waifs and orphans who lived in that scruffy wooden shack at the edge of town.

'Why on earth would they want to kill one of that gang?' asked Redding, even more confused.

'Because they were trying to send a message out from the telegraph office about these gunmen in town.'

Redding stared at Schmidt, stunned.

'What?'

The blacksmith nodded and glared at the Mayor accusingly.

'They were doing what you should have done, Mayor. They were trying to save this town.'

'I don't believe that,' replied Redding, doing his best to appear confident and calm the angry blacksmith. 'Like I told you before, the head gunman has assured me that if we just let them do what they're here to do, they'll just ride out and leave us alone.' He sighed. 'It's unfortunate, and if I could I'd resist them, that you can be sure of, Mr Schmidt. But with the Sheriff locked up in his own jail . . .'

'They're gonna kill us all!' insisted Schmidt, anger rising inside him.

Redding stared at Schmidt, then he laughed. But the blacksmith could hear the nervousness beneath his laugh.

'Really, Mr Schmidt, where did you hear that ridiculous . . .'

'Jess said so,' said Schmidt. 'The boys heard Boone telling it to one of his men. He said they don't want to leave any witnesses, because when they kill the soldiers the army is gonna come looking for 'em.'

The Mayor sat down, shocked, his mind in a whirl.

Surely Boone couldn't possibly intend to kill all the townsfolk . . . it was an impossible thought! Just to silence witnesses to a stage robbery?

But this was not just any stage robbery. This was a gold shipment of a hundred thousand dollars. If it developed into a gunfight, then soldiers of the US army would be killed. When the robbers were caught they'd hang for sure.

Redding felt a sickness clutch at his throat. The Mayor looked at Schmidt, his face white and drawn.

'You're wrong!' insisted Redding. 'This is just some story those boys have invented to stir things up. It's because Boone and his men have locked up the Sheriff in his own jail.' Then a thought struck him. 'In fact, there's proof they're lying!' he said.

'What?' asked Schmidt, frowning.

'If they were going to shoot anyone, they'd have shot the Sheriff,' said Redding. 'But instead they locked him in his own jail. Don't that show they mean what they say? That no one's gonna be harmed?'

'Then why would Jess say such things?' insisted Schmidt stoutly. 'About the gang killing everyone in the town after they've done the robbery?'

'Because he wants to stir up trouble!' repeated the Mayor. 'Those boys have always been troublemakers!'

'Those boys are good and honest workers!' snapped back Schmidt angrily. 'And what about Pete getting shot?'

'Who got shot?' demanded a harsh voice from the doorway.

The Mayor and Schmidt turned. Boone was standing there, with one of his henchmen. Redding felt faint. He wondered how long Boone had been there? How much had he overheard?

'I said who got shot?' shouted Boone angrily, and he pulled his pistol from its holster.

CHAPTER 16

Jess and Billy Joe watched the rear door of the bank from their hiding place behind a pile of packing cases. They'd originally planned to go back to the shack and collect Shane, Andy and Patch; but the need to find out how the Mayor would respond to Schmidt's accusations was too strong. They'd crept to the bank and found a hiding place and waited, ready to talk to Schmidt when he came out. Instead, to their shock and horror, Boone and one of his gunmen had appeared and gone into the bank.

'What'll they do?' asked Billy Joe, nervously.

'Maybe nothing,' whispered back Jess. 'It depends on how angry Mr Schmidt gets.'

'I hope he doesn't get too angry,' admitted Billy Joe. 'Boone will just shoot him dead. And we're fast running out of people who are on our side.'

A movement in the rear door of the bank caught

their attention, and they ducked down behind the packing cases, peering between them to see what was happening. Boone and his henchman stepped out of the bank. Both of them had guns in their hands. In front of them walked the big blacksmith, his hands clasped together behind his head. He looked angry, his big face giving off his silent fury.

'Put him in the jail with the Sheriff,' ordered Boone. 'I'm gonna have me a word with the Mayor.'

Jess and Billy Joe watched as the big blacksmith was marched across the street to the Sheriff's office at gunpoint. They saw Boone turn and go back inside the bank.

'This is gonna go bad, Billy Joe,' murmured Jess. 'My guess is Mr Schmidt told the Mayor about what happened to Pete. The Mayor will tell Boone, and sure as eggs is eggs Boone is gonna check it out. And when he does that, they're gonna come lookin' for us to shut us up.'

'What are we gonna do, Jess?' asked Billy Joe. 'There's no way out of town.'

Jess's face creased into a worried frown as he thought about their situation.

'Trouble is, this town ain't big enough for us to hide in and stay hidden for long. Especially with Andy to think of. And Patch.'

'You ain't thinking of leavin' 'em?' asked Billy Joe, shocked.

Jess looked directly back at Billy Joe and shook his head firmly. Honesty and loyalty were so plain in Jess's eyes, Billy Joe could see why it was the other boys accepted him as their leader with no question.

'No way!' said Jess. 'But we gotta find a way of getting 'em somewhere safe and away from Boone and his men.' He shot a look up and down the street. 'Let's go get 'em somewhere safe before Boone gets to 'em.'

* * *

Boone stood in Redding's office and looked directly at the Mayor. Redding felt like he'd never been so scared in all his life. The look in the outlaw's eyes was pure ice, no feeling at all.

'Let's make sure I got this straight, Mr Mayor,' said Boone. 'Your blacksmith friend . . .'

'He's no friend of mine, I assure you!' said Redding hastily.

'Your blacksmith friend,' continued Boone, ignoring Redding's interruption, his tone firmer and more menacing, 'says this boy got shot up at the telegraph hut. And also that I'm planning to kill everyone in this town after our business here is done. Isn't that what he just said?'

'He didn't mean it,' blustered Redding. 'He's just repeating some tittle-tattle a gang of no-good boys told him.'

'And who do you believe, Mr Mayor? Me, or this gang of boys?'

'You, of course!'

'Good,' said Boone. 'I'd hate to think you might try and double-cross me.'

'I promise I'd never do that!' burst out Redding.

Boone frowned.

'Still, this story of the dead boy makes me curious,' he said.

'Like I say, it's just some made-up tittle-tattle . . .'

'Maybe,' nodded Boone. 'So what we need is for you and me to take a walk to this telegraph hut so you can see there's nothing in that story. Then you can come back and tell that to your friend Schmidt, and anyone else who starts listening to these tall stories. Right, Mr Mayor?'

'Of course!' nodded Redding fervently.

'Good,' said Boone. 'Then let's go see.'

✳ ✳ ✳

Redding walked with Boone out of town and along the track that led to the telegraph hut. All the while Redding had to fight to stop his teeth chattering in fear. He knew all he had to do was keep Boone calm – so long as Boone was calm, the Mayor would stay alive.

As they neared the telegraph hut, everything looked quiet.

'See?' said Boone confidently. 'Everything's nice and normal. Nothing wrong going on here.'

'Absolutely!' agreed Redding fervently. 'I said to myself "Why would anyone want to kill a boy and mess things up when here's so much at stake . . ."'

He stopped as he entered the telegraph hut.

There was a body on the floor. A boy's body.

CHAPTER 17

Redding rushed outside the hut and vomited noisily. Boone glared down at the boy's dead body, then at the telegraph operator sitting behind his desk at the telegraph machine, and finally at the gunman who'd got to his feet as Boone came in.

'What in tarnation happened here, Abbey!' Boone shouted angrily.

'It wasn't my fault, boss!' whined Abbey. 'These kids played a trick on me, pretending there was some sort of fire outside. I took the operator out to make sure he couldn't send any wires, and when I come back there was this kid sitting as large as life in that chair looking like he was sending a message. I showed him my gun and asked him what he thought he was doin', and suddenly this other kid came out of nowhere and jumped on me.'

'So you blew his head off,' scowled Boone.

'I didn't know he was just a kid, I thought he was some grown-up from town who'd come sneaking out here,' protested Abbey.

Boone looked at the dead boy on the floor. He turned to Proctor.

'Is this kid's name Pete?'

The telegraph operator spoke up, his voice angry and accusing.

'Yes,' said Proctor. 'That's Pete all right.' He glowered at Abbey. 'Your gunman murdered a twelve-year-old boy. What a brave man!' he sneered.

'Shut up!' Abbey shouted at Proctor.

Boone gave a rueful sigh.

'OK, Abbey, cut the wire,' he said.

'What?' asked Abbey.

'You heard me. Cut the telegraph wire.'

'But I thought you wanted it left open, so no one would get suspicious that things weren't like they oughta be here?'

'That was before you let yourself be suckered by a bunch of kids,' snapped Boone. 'If they can do it once, they can do it again.' A further thought struck him, 'Do you know if the kid sent a message?'

Abbey shook his head.

'He was still sitting there, trying to do it when I come back in.'

Boone turned his attention to Proctor.

'You. Did the kid send one?'

Proctor shrugged.

'How do I know?' He gestured at Abbey. 'I was outside with him.'

Boone thought it over.

'OK,' he said finally. 'Like I said, cut the telegraph wire, Abbey. Then you come back with me to town.'

Abbey gestured at Proctor.

'What about him?' he asked. 'Shall we bring him with us?'

Boone looked at Proctor for a long moment.

'If we don't have a telegraph we don't need an operator,' said Boone curtly.

* ✳ *

Outside the telegraph hut, the dazed Redding leant against the wooden frame of the hut, trying to get his senses. The boy was dead, exactly as Schmidt had said. So that meant the rest of their story could also be true.

The sound of a gunshot from inside the hut made him jump. Then Boone and Abbey came out. Boone was slipping his pistol back into its holster. Redding backed away fearfully from the gunman, but a scowl from Boone stopped him in his tracks.

'Do you know where these kids live?' he demanded.

Redding gulped, then nodded.

'There's only a handful of them. They live in a shack at the back of town.'

Boone grabbed Redding by the arm, strong fingers digging into the Mayor's arm.

'Show me this shack,' he ordered. Turning to Abbey, he added, 'Abbey, you come with me. We're gonna get rid of some vermin.'

CHAPTER 18

Boone, Abbey and Redding arrived at the edge of town and the tumbledown shack, where the boys lived.

Boone looked at it, at the holes in the roof where cloths had been fixed to keep out the rain, and the pieces of wood nailed to the wooden walls to keep it firm, and sneered.

'One strong gust of wind and this heap will just blow over,' he said.

'Like I said, Mr Boone, these boys are just trash,' said Redding.

'In that case you can be grateful to me for dealing with them,' said Boone.

He looked at Redding, whose face was still death white from the sight of Pete's dead body. Boone once again took the Mayor's arm in a tight grip, making Redding wince with pain.

'Now listen, Mr Mayor,' he said. 'You keep quiet about what you saw out at the telegraph hut. If I hear any word about it from the townsfolk, I'll know it came from you. And if that happens, you are a dead man. But if you do as I say and just keep everyone and everything here calm, you'll stay alive. You got it?'

Redding nodded.

'Yes,' he said, his voice barely above a frightened whisper.

'OK,' said Boone. 'You better get back to your bank. We don't want people worrying where you are today, especially with the shipment coming in just over an hour.'

Redding nodded and backed away, then turned and hurried, almost running, back towards his bank.

As he hurried along the Main Street his mind was in a whirl as he thought about the dead body, the shot from inside the telegraph hut and what Schmidt had said the boys had overheard. Boone and his men intended to kill everyone in the town! To commit murder on that scale was unbelievable! Then he thought about what had happened so far, things he had seen with his own eyes, and he knew the boys were right.

'I have to get out of here,' he whispered to himself, then he shot a nervous look around, worried he might have been overheard. He hadn't intended to say the words aloud.

✳ ✳ ✳

Abbey and Boone watched the Mayor disappear along the Main Street.

'That's one frightened man, boss,' said Abbey.

'And he'd better stay frightened,' growled Boone.

He drew his gun and went towards the door.

'OK, let's go hunt us some kids.'

He kicked open the door of the shack and stepped inside. Abbey followed him, guns also drawn.

The two men looked around the one room shack.

'There's no one here,' said Abbey.

'That's just how it looks,' grated Boone. 'They're hiding. It's what I'd be doing if I was them.'

Boone stood listening intently, straining his ears for any sound, perhaps the shuffling sound of someone moving beneath a blanket, or breathing.

Suddenly he heard it. A movement behind a pile of blankets. That was where they were! He let fire with his pistols into the pile of blankets, the bullets tearing into the blankets and scattering shredded cloth, and three terrified mice ran from behind the blankets and headed for the door.

'Mice!' chuckled Abbey.

'It don't mean those kids ain't still hiding here,' snarled Boone.

'You think I should search around?' asked Abbey.

Boone shook his head.

'These kids are too slippery. Get near 'em, they're as likely to slip by you. No, there's only one way to find out if they're hiding in here.'

With that Boone levelled both his guns and began to fire around the room in a scatter pattern. The sound of the shots in the small shack was deafening. As the bullets from Boone's guns tore into the walls and the furniture, slivers of wood flew around. Finally, the hammer of Boone's guns clicked on empty chambers. Boone began reloading.

'OK,' he told Abbey. 'Now you can search.'

Abbey began roaming inside the small shack, pulling at the drapes, kicking chairs aside, turning over cushions and blankets. All the time Boone stood in the doorway, guns drawn, ready to start firing if any of the boys appeared and made a run for the door.

Finally, Abbey rejoined Boone, shaking his head.

'They're not here,' he said.

'No, but they're somewhere in town,' mused Boone.

'You want us to find 'em?' asked Abbey. 'Lock 'em up?'

Boone shook his head.

'I want you to take a few of the men and find 'em and kill 'em,' he said. 'That's the only way to make sure we shut 'em up.' He looked at Abbey and grinned. 'It shouldn't be too hard for you. You've already shot one kid today.'

'That was an accident!' said Abbey defensively.

Boone shrugged.

'Don't fret none,' he said. 'We'll be killing a whole heap of kids and women later.'

'But say the townsfolk get to hear about us killing the kids . . .' began Abbey.

'They ain't going to,' said Boone. 'And even if they do, it don't matter. I want you to send some of our boys and start rounding the townsfolk up. They're to take 'em to the saloon. If any of 'em have got guns, take them off 'em. Leave the three Tucker brothers, Charlie Moss and Danno in the saloon guarding them – they can be trusted to do things right.'

'Say the people won't go to the saloon?' asked Abbey.

'It's up to you boys to make sure they do,' said Boone looking up and giving a cold, hard grin. 'I'm sure you and the boys can be real persuasive. If they play up, take 'em somewhere and shoot 'em. We ain't got time for playing nice.'

He pulled a watch from his pocket and studied it.

'Eleven o'clock,' he announced. 'If it's on time, the stage with the gold on it should be arriving in just about an hour. That'll give time to get the townsfolk safe in the saloon.

'And don't be too long finding those kids. I want them dead within half an hour, so you can join the rest of the boys in the bank. Got that?'

'If you ask me, boss, it's all leavin' it late. We should've put the townsfolk in the saloon first thing this morning.' Abbey said, frowning.

Boone gave Abbey a dangerous look.

'Are you questionin' my decision?' he demanded, tight-lipped, and Abbey saw the spark of anger in Boone's eyes. He'd seen that same look before, usually just before Boone killed someone.

'No no, boss,' gulped Abbey hastily. 'It's just . . .'

'If we'd stuck 'em all in the saloon first thing, by now they'd have bin moanin' and complainin', and maybe some of 'em might even have started to get the others all fired up about how it ain't right,' snapped Boone. 'Pretty soon we'd have had a riot on our hands and someone would've got shot, and then we'd have more trouble on our hands instead of gettin' on with the robbery. Keepin' them apart, and then puttin' them in the saloon just for an hour or so, they'll all be nice and well-behaved.

'It would have all bin fine if it hadn't bin for those kids sneakin' around causin' trouble. I don't want them causin' any more mess. That's why you better make sure you find 'em and deal with 'em.'

'Don't worry, boss,' nodded Abbey. 'I'll find them and have them dead before they know what's hit 'em.'

CHAPTER 19

Billy Joe, Shane and Andy crouched in the low-roofed loft above Mr Schmidt's blacksmith forge. Patch lay down with them. He didn't know what was happening, but he knew whatever it was wasn't good – the boys could tell from the worried expression in the dog's eyes.

A noise from the ladder that led up from the forge below made them start, and Shane picked up a pitchfork he'd found and levelled it at the loft opening, reading to thrust it forward, but the face that appeared was Jess's.

Shane put down the sharp pitchfork with a gasp of relief.

'You sh-shoulda said it w-was you!' he complained.

Jess clambered up through the loft opening and joined the other boys.

'Yeah?' he queried. 'And say Boone's men were up

here instead and I called out my name? What would have happened then?'

'They ain't been here,' said Billy Joe.

'We-we heard shootin',' said Shane. 'W-we thought it was you.'

'It was our shack,' said Jess. 'It looks like we got out just in time. I watched from a distance. They shot the place up pretty bad. I guess they're out right now looking for us.' He pulled out his pocket watch and looked at the time. 'My hope is they'll be too busy gettin' ready for the stage. There's only about an hour before it gets here.'

'So if we stay hidden here for an hour then all of us will be safe?' piped up Andy hopefully, and he patted Patch.

'Maybe,' shrugged Jess. 'But then again, maybe once they've robbed the stage and got the money, they'll take time to check everywhere in this town to make sure they don't leave any witnesses alive.'

'We're gonna have to make a run for it,' said Billy Joe. 'Way I see it, we wait till the shooting starts and then we just head out of town as quick as we can and hide in a gulley somewhere. Then, when they've gone, we start running and keep running.'

'They'll kill the Sheriff and Mr Schmidt and everyone else who's been good to us,' said Jess sternly. 'We got to do our best to stop that happening.'

'We can't!' protested Billy Joe. 'We can't even save

ourselves! Pete got shot. We're hiding up here. If we try and stop Boone and his gang we'll die for sure.'

'I don't care,' said Jess. 'Like I said, these people have been good to me. I owe them.'

'Not all of them!' persisted Billy Joe, his eyes on Jess. 'I don't know all these people in this town, but it seems to me people like the Mayor couldn't care if you live or die, so you don't owe those people anything at all!'

'That don't matter,' said Jess. 'I aim to help the people I owe. And if that means going up against Boone, and maybe getting myself killed, then so be it.' He sighed. 'But I accept this ain't your fight, Billy Joe. You only came to Drygulch last night, and straight away your pa got shot dead. You don't owe anybody here anything.'

'He o-o-owes you,' said Shane. 'You s-saved his life l-l-last n-night.'

Jess shook his head.

'I just did what anybody else would have done,' he said. 'As far as I'm concerned Billy Joe can make a run for it with no hard feelings. Me, I'm gonna see if I can save the Sheriff and Mr Schmidt. And I'm also remembering that these people killed Pete. I aim to see them hang for that.' He looked around at the other boys. 'So, Shane and Andy, if you want to try your luck and make a run for it with Billy Joe, that's fine by me. But me, I'm staying here.'

There was an uncomfortable silence, before Shane said, 'I'm s-staying. P-Pete got killed cos of me. I w-wanna put that right. He was my b-brother.'

Jess hesitated, then nodded.

'OK,' he said. Turning to Billy Joe, he said, 'But somebody's got to look after Andy. Will you do that, Billy Joe? Take him with you when you go?'

Before Billy Joe could reply, Andy spoke up very firmly, 'I ain't goin. We're family.'

With that he reached out and ruffled the fur of Patch's ears. Patch looked up, hopefully.

'And Patch says he wants to stay, too,' he added.

'OK,' Jess nodded. 'Right, Billy Joe. Looks like you're gonna be on your own. But if you do get away, make sure you tell the people outside we wasn't all cowards like Mayor Redding. That some of us stood up to Boone and his gang.'

Billy Joe sighed, a long sad sigh.

'I guess someone else is gonna have to do that,' he said. 'If anyone manages to get out of here, that is.'

Andy's eyes lit up.

'You mean you're staying, Billy Joe?' he asked.

Billy Joe nodded, looking round at the boys.

'My pa's dead,' he said. 'You all took me in. I guess here is as good a place to stay as any.'

Jess regarded Billy Joe doubtfully.

'There's a sure chance of you getting killed if you stay,' he said.

Billy Joe shrugged.

'There's a chance I'll get killed trying to run,' he said softly. 'If I'm gonna die, I might as well die with an easy mind.'

CHAPTER 20

In the jail, Sheriff Nolan pulled his watch from his waistcoat pocket.

'What's the time, Sheriff?' asked Schmidt.

'A quarter after eleven,' said Nolan. He closed his watch and slipped it back into his waistcoat pocket.

He felt helpless. He cursed himself for having been caught out by the gunmen and being thrown into his own jail like this. But a sense of cold reason told him there had been nothing else he could do, not against five armed men. If he'd resisted, they'd have simply shot him dead. At least this way he was alive, and while he was alive there was always a chance he could stop the robbery. Or, even if he couldn't stop the robbery, there was a hope he could save some of the townsfolk.

He reflected on what Schmidt had told him about the robbers' plans to kill all the townspeople, and he knew that the blacksmith was right. He'd known it when he'd looked Boone in the face and seen the emptiness of feelings in those eyes. Boone was like a machine. People didn't matter to him. It was all about the money. And the power created by his gun.

'Stage is due in under an hour,' said Schmidt.

'Maybe it'll be late,' said Nolan. 'It often is.'

'It don't matter when it arrives,' said Schmidt. 'Boone and his men are still gonna rob it and kill all the soldiers. And after, they're gonna kill everyone else to make sure there's no witnesses.' He looked around at the cell they were in: the strong thick iron bars cemented from floor to ceiling. 'It's a pity you made this jail so hard to break out of, Sheriff. Even I couldn't bend these bars apart.'

Nolan sat down on the bench and studied the construction of the cell. It was the thousandth time he'd done it since he'd been locked in here. The iron bars with the cell door in it that led out to the Sheriff's office. One window high up in the wall, also with iron bars in it, that let light in from the other side of the jail, from the back road. The walls of the jail were solid brick, so there was no chance of kicking them out, like there might be with most of the timber buildings in Drygulch.

'If only we could get one of those gunmen into the cell,' he mused. 'Maybe we could pretend that one of us is dying. Then we could jump him.'

Schmidt shook his head.

'They ain't gonna do that,' he said. 'They ain't that stupid. And even if they are, they still ain't gonna come in here. Not until they're ready to kill us. And then they won't bother to open the cell door, they'll just shoot us through those bars.' He sighed. 'Our only hope is those soldiers will put up a fight and maybe win.'

'Ten soldiers against forty armed killers?' queried Nolan. 'Plus, the soldiers don't know they're riding into an ambush.' He gave an angry sigh. 'It'll be like shooting fish in a barrel.'

The huge bar at the saloon was filling up as more and more of the townsfolk were escorted in by Boone's gunmen. Some came quietly, disturbed by these dirty dust-stained men with well-used guns in their hands. They sat down at the tables and murmured and whispered quietly together, talking in worried tones about what was happening in their town.

Others complained.

Old Mr Pantages, who owned the hardware store, was one of them.

'This ain't right!' he growled as the gunman guided him through the swinging bat-wing doors into the saloon. 'We was told everything would go on as usual! The Mayor told us so!'

'And now the Mayor's worried about you people getting hurt,' said the gunman.

'I ain't gonna get hurt!' snapped Pantages. 'I ain't that stupid! As soon as I see the stage comin', I'm gonna take myself upstairs and lock myself in.'

The gunman shook his head.

'Look, I'm just following orders. Everybody's got to be here together, so we know that everyone is safe. We don't want no one out on the street where they might get hurt.'

'This ain't what we was promised,' grumbled Pantages. 'We was told to carry on our regular business and everything would be fine.'

The gunman scowled. This was getting boring. He felt like shooting the old man right here and now to shut him up. But he remembered the instructions Abbey had given him, about shooting people away from sight, so not to upset things and make them worse.

'Look, old timer, if you're really upset about this, you can always come and talk to my boss and make your complaint to him.'

Pantages thought about it.

'Where is this boss of yours?'

'At the livery stable,' said the gunman. In his mind he was already shooting the hardware store owner and leaving his dead body in one of the stables.

Pantages shook his head.

'Nope,' he said. 'I can't be bothered to walk all that way, not with my aches and pains in my legs. I guess I'll make my feelings known to him after.'

The gunman nodded.

'You do that,' he said.

He scowled as he watched the store-owner walk away. The old guy had irritated him. This waiting irritated him. He wanted something to happen. Shooting the store-owner would have been doing something.

Pantages ambled to a table where his old friends, Amos and Amy Johnson and their fifteen-year old daughter, Priscilla, were sitting. He sat down and joined them.

'This is the biggest nuisance I ever saw,' he told them.

Mrs Johnson nodded, her lips prim and set.

'That's exactly what I said to the young man who came and fetched us,' she said. 'I told him, why can't we stay in our own home? We don't plan to cause any trouble.'

'Exactly what I said,' nodded Pantages. He looked round the room, with its glass chandeliers and its long bar. It was already filled, with more people coming in all the time. As he watched, the doors swung open and the preacher and his wife and seven children came in. They looked around them at the saloon, expressions of distaste plain on their faces. Pantages chuckled.

'I bet that's the first time Preacher Varley and his family have ever set foot in this unholy place,' he grinned.

'And I bet it'll be the last, too,' agreed Mr Johnson.

CHAPTER 21

In the loft of the blacksmith's forge, the boys peered out through the hatch. Outside, the town sounded quiet. *The quiet before the storm*, thought Billy Joe. He'd heard his pa say that when things got too quiet.

Jess pulled out his watch, opened the face on it and checked the time. 'The stage is gonna be here very soon,' he said. 'I guess maybe it's time for us to make a move.'

'W-what w-we gonna do, Jess?' asked Shane.

Jess sighed. 'I don't rightly know,' he admitted. 'Until we get down from here and find out where everyone is, we can't make a plan.'

Billy Joe gestured at Jess's watch.

'That sure is a mighty fine watch,' he said, impressed. 'Where d'you get it?'

'It was my pa's,' said Jess. He slipped it back in his

pocket. 'That and the hat I lent you, that's all I got of him. But it's good to have something of his.'

Billy Joe shrugged.

'I ain't got nothin' of my pa's,' he said.

'We all got something, Billy Joe, even if it's just a memory,' said Jess quietly. 'Anyway, let's get down and see what's going on . . .'

Suddenly he froze, alert, his finger to his lips. The other boys stopped as well. There were footsteps coming into the forge from the street. The sound of boots. And voices.

Hastily, the boys crept back from the loft opening.

'Them boys ain't here, Abbey,' complained one man. 'We practically tore this town apart looking for them. They weren't at the livery stable. They weren't at the hardware store. They weren't at the drugstore . . .'

'We bin lookin' in the wrong place!' Abbey told him. 'It was starin' us in the face the whole time! This is where they are!'

Billy Joe and Shane exchanged glances – they'd know that voice anywhere!

'Why are you so sure they're gonna be hiding here at the blacksmith's?' demanded another voice.

'Because the boys went to see the blacksmith and told him about what happened at the telegraph hut,' said Abbey. 'That means they know him well. They know he's in the jail, so his forge is the best place for them to hide.'

Billy Joe leaned forward slowly and peered down through a crack in the wooden floor of the loft. The cowboy, the one that shot Pete, was gesturing around at the forge, at all the tools and the cupboards. 'You guys start looking in there!' He pulled his gun from its holster. 'Me, I'm goin' up and take a look in that loft.'

While the other two cowboys began searching through the cupboards and piles of timber in the forge, Abbey walked to the ladder and grabbed hold of it, ready to haul himself up. Immediately, Shane grabbed up the pitchfork again, but all the boys knew one pitchfork would be no use against three armed men.

Jess looked around for something, anything, to use as a weapon, as he heard Abbey's boots creak on the ladder.

'Abbey!'

The shout came from outside.

Billy Joe struggled to get a better view of what was happening through the floorboards. Another of the bandits had run into the forge from the street.

Abbey stopped climbing the ladder and scowled. The other two cowboys had stopped their searching.

'What?' demanded Abbey.

'Boone's calling for you,' said the new arrival, his tone urgent.

'He told me he wants us to find these kids,' said Abbey.

The man shook his head.

'He said you're taking too long. The stage is due soon. He wants you in the bank with the others. They've got all the townsfolk rounded up in the saloon.'

Abbey looked up at the loft opening, his gun drawn.

'Tell him we'll be along as soon as we've done what we're doing,' he said.

The man looked doubtful and nervous.

'I ain't sayin' any such thing like that to Boone,' he said. 'If you want him to hear that, you tell him yourself. He ain't in a good mood at the moment.'

Abbey hesitated. He knew what Boone was like in a bad mood. It didn't do to upset Boone.

'OK,' he said, resigned. 'We're coming.'

He dropped down from the ladder, and then he and the other cowboys hurried out of the forge and headed towards the bank.

Billy Joe moved away from the crack in the floor of the loft and let out a long breath of relief.

'That sure was lucky!' he said. 'I thought we were gonna be caught for sure!'

'S-seems like they rounded up the whole t-town up, 'cept us,' said Shane. He looked helplessly at Jess, and then he began to cry. Jess went to him and put his arm round Shane's shoulders.

'Keep strong, Shane,' he said. 'We'll get out of this somehow.'

Shane shook his head.

'I'm c-c-cryin' cos th-that's the man who sh-shot Pete,' he said. 'I sh-shoulda killed him j-just now, but I d-didn't.'

Jess nodded in understanding.

'We'll get justice for Pete, I promise, Shane,' he said.

'But what we gonna do now, Jess?' asked Billy Joe.

Jess frowned thoughtfully.

'The only man who could even think about stopping this is the Sheriff, and he's in jail,' he reminded them.

'If we had a gun,' said Billy Joe. 'we could sneak it in through the window of the jail and give it to the Sheriff and he could shoot his way out.'

'Oh yeah?' said Shane sarcastically. 'One m-m-man against forty g-gunmen?'

'He could maybe fire a warning shot to warn the stage before it gets to the bank,' said Billy Joe.

The boys looked at one another, excited at this new idea.

'That's g-good thinkin' there, B-Billy Joe,' admitted Shane, then he sighed. 'But we ain't g-got a g-gun!'

'No, but Mr Schmidt has,' said Jess sharply, suddenly remembering. 'He don't wear it, but he keeps one stashed away just in case of trouble. It's in one of the cupboards in his forge. I'm pretty sure it's at the back of one of the cupboards near the fire.'

'W-what are we w-waiting for?' said an excited Shane. 'Let's l-look for it!'

'Yeah!' said Andy delightedly, getting to his feet.

'No, Andy,' said Jess firmly. 'You stay up here.'

Andy looked at Jess in dismay.

'Why?' he complained. 'Just cos I'm the littlest! I can do things! I work!'

'I know you do, Andy' said Jess. 'But someone's got to look after Patch and make sure he don't climb down and go out on the street. He could get shot and killed. Patch needs you to make sure he stays up here and alive.'

Andy hesitated, torn between staying in the loft and helping the bigger boys. He looked at Patch, who wagged his tail and came over to Andy. Andy looked at Jess and nodded.

'OK,' he said.

He put his arms around the dog's neck.

'I'll make sure he don't go nowhere,' he told the three older boys.

Jess peered over the edge of the loft opening.

'It all looks clear,' he said. 'Let me check.'

Jess went carefully down the wooden ladder to ground level. He crept along the wall of the forge and peered out into the Main Street.

It was empty except for the two men, Scar and Moustache, still sitting outside the Sheriff's office.

Further along the street were the bank and the saloon, where the gunman and the townspeople were gathered inside.

'OK!' Jess called up in a loud whisper. 'All clear!'

Billy Joe and Shane slid quickly down the ladder. While Billy Joe acted as a lookout, Jess and Shane began searching through the cupboards in the blacksmith's forge.

It was Shane who found the gun. It was at the back of the cupboard nearest the blacksmith's anvil.

'G-g-got it!' he said triumphantly.

Jess took it from him and checked it. It had a full round of six bullets in the chamber.

'Good,' he said. 'Now we got to get it to the Sheriff.'

'Me and Shane can do that,' said Billy Joe. 'We'll do it the way we spoke to the Sheriff before. We'll go to the window at the back and Shane gets on my shoulders and pushes the gun through the bars on the window.'

Jess shook his head.

'It's dangerous. I should be doin' it.'

'No it ain't,' said Billy Joe. 'Most everybody's off the streets now so we shouldn't be seen. The dangerous part is the other bit.'

'W-what other b-bit?' asked Shane, puzzled.

'The bit where Jess goes in and gets the keys to the jail, after the Sheriff's shot those two gunmen dead.'

Jess looked at Billy Joe and grinned.

'That's smart thinking, Billy Joe,' he said. 'You got some clever sneakiness in you.'

'I learnt it from my pa,' said Billy Joe. And, to his surprise, he suddenly felt a lump in his throat as he thought of his father and he felt tears well up in his eyes. Hastily, he blinked to get rid of them.

If Jess noticed Billy Joe's tears he didn't say anything about them. He simply nodded.

'I'll hide round the corner of the Sheriff's office. As soon as I hear shooting, I'll go in.' He held out his hand, and Shane and Billy Joe added theirs to his, and gripped each other's hands firmly.

'We gotta do this right,' said Jess. 'But most of all, we gotta stay alive. We don't want no more of us being killed. We owe it to Pete.'

CHAPTER 22

Jess, Billy Joe and Shane crept along the back lane behind the blacksmith's forge until they came to the livery stable at the far end of town. Using the bales of straw stacked along the livery stable's fence as cover, they crept across to the other side of the Main Street.

All the while they were aware how eerily quiet the town was. Apart from the two gunmen sitting on the boardwalk outside the Sheriff's office, the three boys were the only people on the street.

They hurried along a back lane. When they got to the alleyway that led to the Main Street by the Sheriff's office, Jess stopped and slid beneath the wooden boardwalk, ready and waiting.

He watched Shane and Billy Joe get to the barred window at the back of the jail.

It couldn't be long before the stagecoach with the

gold got there. *Let's hope the Sheriff gets out in time*, Jess thought.

Inside the jail, Sheriff Nolan paced up and down the cell. Schmidt sat on the bunk and watched him.

'Walking up and down like that ain't gonna get us out of here, Sheriff,' he said.

'Maybe not, but I feel I gotta do something,' growled the Sheriff.

In all his time as a lawman he'd never felt so helpless. Suddenly he heard a scratching sound from the barred window, and a whispered voice calling his name. He looked up. A pistol had been pushed through the bars.

The Sheriff reached up and took hold of the pistol. He could just make out Shane's fair hair through the bars, and then the boy dropped out of sight.

Schmidt had got up from the bunk and joined Nolan. He stared at the pistol in the Sheriff's hand with a shock of recognition.

'That's my gun!' he said.

'Does it work?' asked Nolan.

'It sure do!' said Schmidt proudly. 'I keep it oiled and in good working order, just in case I need to use it.'

The Sheriff and Schmidt exchanged glances. They were going to need it now.

'Right,' said the Sheriff. 'Maybe at last we've got a chance to stop those gunmen!' He thought quickly, then said to Schmidt, 'Lay down on the bunk and start groaning.'

'Why?' asked the blacksmith.

'Just do as I tell you, Otto!' said Nolan impatiently.

Schmidt lay down on the bunk and started to groan, as if he was in pain.

Hiding the pistol behind his back, Sheriff Nolan he called out, 'Hey! Help! He's dying!'

There was no reaction from the two men sitting outside.

Nolan shouted louder.

'Hey! Help! We need help!'

There was a scuffling noise, then the door of the Sheriff's office opened and one of the gunmen appeared. It was the man with the scar.

'Shut your noise!' Scar said tersely.

'But he's in real bad pain!' insisted Nolan, pointing at the groaning man lying on the bunk. 'He's dying!'

'Let him die!' snapped Scar. He turned to leave. As he did so, Nolan pulled the gun from behind his back, aimed it through the bars and fired.

The man with the scarred face gave a yell and collapsed to the floor.

Immediately, the door to the street was kicked open and the gunman with the moustache rushed in, gun in hand. He looked down at Scar lying on the floor who lay there with a look of shock on his face. Then he gave a snarl and raised his gun at the jail cell.

Nolan beat him to it. His shot hit Moustache in the chest.

Moustache sank to the floor.

Schmidt leapt off the bunk and joined Nolan at the bars of the jail cell.

'What do we do now?' he demanded angrily. 'They're dead, but we're still stuck in here!'

'Not for long!' said a voice.

Both men looked and saw that Jess had slipped in from the street.

'Get the key to this cell, Jess!' said the Sheriff urgently.

'That's what I'm here for,' grinned Jess.

He went to the wooden box on the wall next to the 'Wanted' posters, where he knew the Sheriff kept his keys. He opened the box, reached in and took out the heavy key-ring. As he did so, he heard heavy footsteps behind him.

'Stand right there!' snapped a voice.

It was Abbey, Boone's gunman. The one who had shot Pete.

CHAPTER 23

The Sheriff fired at Abbey, but missed as the man threw himself to one side and returned fire. The Sheriff leapt away from the bars as Abbey's bullets poured through, just missing the men inside.

Abbey took cover behind the Sheriff's desk. As Jess tried to run for the cell with the keys, Abbey let fly with a shot that hit the boy in the leg. Jess collapsed to the floor, howling in agony.

'Drop the gun, Sheriff, or my next bullet blows that kid's head off!' ordered Abbey.

Three other gunmen appeared in the doorway, all with their guns drawn. The Sheriff fired and one of the men collapsed backwards out of the door with a yell of pain. The other men jumped back out of the Sheriff's office to seek cover on the street outside.

Jess lay on the floor, biting his lip against the pain in his shattered leg. He fumbled with the keys. If he could just get the key to the cell off the ring! He knew which one it was from helping the Sheriff clean out the cells. Fighting against the pain that tore through him from his broken leg, Jess pressed his thumbs against the catch of the key ring, and some of the keys fell off onto the floor.

Abbey fired a bullet that smacked into the wooden floor near the keys, sending wooden splinters flying up into Jess's face.

'Leave them keys alone, boy!' he snarled. 'I already killed one kid today. I'd rather not kill another, but I will if I have to. You just leave them keys alone and stay right where you are.'

'You won't get away with this!' snapped Nolan. 'The law will hunt you down and find you and hang you! Every one of you!'

'Seems to me we're getting away with it OK so far,' said Abbey. From his hiding place behind the desk, he called out, 'Listen clearly to me, Sheriff. If this was Boone here instead of me you'd all be dead right now. But I ain't no natural killer. Shooting that boy today was an accident. But it happened, and there ain't nothin' I can do about it. Now I can shoot you and the boy and your friend in the cell with you, but that's gonna be messy and the townsfolk are gonna get curious. So why don't you just throw your gun out through the bars and we'll leave it at that.'

'You ain't gonna leave it at that!' accused Nolan.

'You're gonna kill us all once you've robbed the stage!'

'I guess we are at that,' admitted Abbey. 'But how soon do you want to die, Sheriff? Right this minute? Or maybe you'd like to grab another half hour to live, and maybe give yourself and this boy a chance.'

Jess gritted his teeth against the pain and took advantage of this exchange between the men to push the cell key under the corner of the coloured rag-rug. It was the only piece of ornamentation in the Sheriff's office. So long as that key stayed there, hidden from the bandits, there was a chance. The rest of the keys lay where they had fallen. Some on the key-ring, some scattered on the floor. He hoped the Sheriff had spotted him hiding the key.

'I ain't got time to waste, Sheriff,' said Abbey. 'The stage must be almost here by now. I'll count to three. If that gun of yours ain't been thrown through those bars by the time I get to three, the boy dies. One.'

Nolan looked at Jess on the floor, holding his shattered bleeding leg, his face twisted in pain.

'Two.'

Jess turned his face towards Nolan and looked at the Sheriff.

'Don't do it, Sheriff,' he said. 'I don't mind dying.'

'Three.'

Nolan heard the hammer of Abbey's gun click back . . . and he threw his own pistol out through the bars.

'Good,' said Abbey.

He stepped out from behind the cover of the desk and called. The gunmen waiting outside hurried in. Abbey gestured at Jess on the floor.

'Jake and Matt, pick up the boy.'

The men looked at Jess, puzzled frowns on their faces.

'Why?' asked one. 'Might as well shoot him now.'

'I said pick him up!' repeated Abbey firmly. 'Then take him over to the saloon and put him in there with the others.'

As the two men reached down and lifted him up, Jess yelled out with the pain in his leg. Then he bit his lip to try and stop himself yelling out again. He was determined to show these men he didn't cry that easy, not even with a shattered leg. And he'd managed to hide the key. The question now was: had the Sheriff seen him do it? And, even if he had, could he get hold of it?

The two men carried Jess out, and headed towards the saloon. Abbey turned to the remaining gunman. 'Carl, you stay outside on the street and keep an eye on things. Stop anyone else coming in here.'

Carl pointed at the bodies of Scar and Moustache.

'What about them?' he asked.

Abbey shrugged.

'Leave 'em where they are,' he said. 'They ain't goin' no place.'

As Carl went outside to take his place in one of the

chairs outside the Sheriff's office, Abbey bent down and picked up Schmidt's pistol.

'Nice gun,' he commented approvingly.

'I hope it blows up in your hand,' snapped Nolan.

Abbey grinned.

'I guess we'll find that out when I come back and shoot you,' he said.

He bent down, picked up the scattered keys from the floor and slipped them into his pockets.

'Think I'll take these as well,' he said. 'Just in case you got anyone else hanging around you think is gonna help you.'

CHAPTER 24

Billy Joe and Shane watched from their hiding place beneath the boardwalk as Jess was carried out of the Sheriff's office towards the saloon. Shortly after, Abbey, a man they knew all too well, came out and headed for the bank.

'Th-that's the man who shot Pete!' raged Shane, and he leapt to his feet and would have run after Abbey if Billy Joe hadn't grabbed him and pulled him back.

'What d'you think you're doing?!' he demanded angrily. 'He'd have killed you as soon as he saw you comin' at him!'

Shane's face crumpled.

'I d-don't know!' he sniffled. 'I saw him and I just w-w-wanted to get him for killing P-Pete!'

'All in good time,' said Billy Joe. 'We ain't gonna do nothin' good if we get ourselves killed!'

Shane nodded, his face a picture of misery.

'Th-think the Sh-Sheriff and Mr Sch-Schmidt are dead in there?' he asked.

'I don't know,' Billy Joe admitted.

Suddenly, lying there, they heard the thunderous sound of hooves and rolling iron wheels coming from the edge of town. They looked up to see the dust cloud approaching about a quarter of a mile away.

'It's the st-st-stage and the s-s-soldiers,' said Shane. His face tightened and a determined look appeared on his face. 'I ain't g-gonna let this happen!' he said. 'They had no r-right to k-kill P-Pete. I ain't g-gonna let them do this!'

Before Billy Joe could stop him, Shane slid out from beneath the boardwalk, into the side lane, then ran towards the back lane. Billy Joe groaned in frustration at this. He slid along the ground and out from under the boardwalk. He was just about to hurry after Shane, when an angry shout from the gunman outside the Sheriff's office, made him stop.

'What in tarnation are you doing?!' the man yelled.

Billy Joe looked in the direction the gunman was shouting and was shocked to see Patch running along the Main Street, with Andy running after him shouting 'Patch! Come here!'

'Andy!' yelled Billy Joe urgently. 'Get off the street! Now!'

Carl the gunman looked shock as he realized the shout had come from the lane at the side of Sheriff's office. He pulled his gun, spun towards Billy Joe and fired. But Billy Joe was already running, zig-zagging across the lane, bullets smacking into the dusty ground around him as he ran.

Billy Joe made it to far side of the lane and threw himself round the corner, just in time as more bullets smashed into the wooden buildings near him.

The gunman turned back towards the Main Street, cursing. Where were the little kid and the dog? But they had vanished from sight.

Carl knew he ought to go after them, look for them. But he could hear the crash and clatter of the wheels of the stagecoach, the horses' hooves, and the clank of the cavalry's saddlery and swords as the convoy got nearer and nearer. At any second it would be round the bend in the street and heading for the bank.

And there it was! The stagecoach pulled by a team of four horses, steam coming off them. High up on the front box of the stagecoach were the driver and his partner riding shotgun. Behind them came ten mounted cavalry soldiers, riding in pairs. Their blue uniforms were stained white and grey from the dust on the road, as were the coats of their horses. In just a minute they would be pulling up outside the bank, and . . .

'S-stop! Ambush!'

The cowboy's mouth opened in shock as he saw the short stocky figure of a fair-haired boy in buckskin appear from one of the back streets and run right into the path of the stagecoach, waving his arms.

This couldn't be happening!

Boone's man pulled his gun from his holster and levelled it at the boy, but there was no need. The horses pulling the stagecoach were going to run the boy down and trample him for sure.

CHAPTER 25

Shane stood there in the middle of the street, feeling the ground beneath his feet shake as the horses and the stagecoach bore down on him getting ever nearer. He could see the stagecoach driver pulling frantically at the reins and at the same time pulling on the brake. One of the mounted soldiers overtook the stagecoach and pulled his horse to a halt beside Shane.

'Get out of the way, kid!' he yelled angrily.

Shane stood his ground as the coach slid to a standstill and he pointed towards the bank.

'It's an am-m-bush!' he yelled. 'There are g-gunmen hiding in the bank, and the p-places opposite!'

'What?'

The soldier looked momentarily shocked, then comprehension dawned on his face. He turned towards the rest of the troop of soldiers, who had pulled up their horses.

'Robbers!' he called. 'Group up around the stage!'

The ten cavalrymen pulled their horses around the stagecoach. Two of the soldiers jumped onto the roof of the stage to join the driver and his partner.

Even as they did so, the doors of the bank burst open and Boone's gunmen came out, pistols and rifles ablaze. The soldiers returned fire, and the first row of gunmen tumbled into the dust and onto the boardwalk.

* * *

Inside the Golden Dollar saloon everyone was gathered round the injured Jess, who'd been dumped on the floor. Everyone, that is, except the four armed gunmen standing around the walls, keeping watch on the townsfolk inside the saloon.

Mrs Johnson was already tearing a tablecloth into strips to use for bandages.

'Go and get some whiskey from the bar,' she ordered her husband. She looked down at Jess, who was pale-faced and groaning. 'When I start tying his leg up, he's gonna need something to stop the pain from kicking in.'

Old Mr Pantages stormed away from Jess and confronted the gunman nearest the door.

'Where in tarnation do you come from shooting a boy like that!' he demanded angrily.

The gunman returned Pantages's glare with a glare of his own.

'It wasn't me who shot him,' he snapped. 'And my guess is whoever did had a reason for doin' so. Now get out of my face before I shoot you myself!'

Pantages glowered at the gunman and an angry retort sprang to his lips, but as he saw the gunman reach for the pistol in his belt, Pantages stopped himself. Instead, he returned to where Mrs and Priscilla Johnson had torn the leg of Jess's trousers to expose the wound.

'I sure wish I had my scissors,' sighed Mrs Johnson.

Mr Johnson returned from the bar with a bottle of whiskey.

'Here,' he said, holding it out to his wife.

She took it and looked at Jess.

'This is gonna hurt, son,' she said. 'I'm gonna splash it on the wound to clean it so it don't get infected . . .'

Jess gritted his teeth against the pain, and muttered something that Mrs Johnson couldn't make out.

'What?' she asked. 'I can't hear you, son.'

Jess did his best to struggle up on his elbow, though every movement sent a wave of pain through his body.

'They're gonna kill us all,' he said. 'Once they've robbed the stage, they're gonna kill us all.'

As he said these words, the sound of gunfire erupted from outside in the street, rifles and pistols bursting bullets and flame.

* * *

Billy Joe stayed under cover beneath the wooden boardwalk and watched the battle raging further down the street. Where was Shane? He'd seen Shane run out and stop the stage and the soldiers, and the next second everything had broken out as the gunmen poured out of the bank and the buildings opposite.

The man standing outside the Sheriff's office, gun in hand, was hopping about like a man who wasn't sure what to do. This wasn't going to plan. As more of the gunmen fell to the ground from the soldier's bullets, he made his mind up and ran forward to join the gunfight, pistols in both hands, firing.

Billy Joe took the opportunity. He slid out from beneath the boardwalk and ran to the Sheriff's office, keeping low and zig-zagging in case anyone saw him and took a shot. But all the gunmen's attention was on the stage and the soldiers.

Billy Joe ran through the door and fell over the body of Scar just inside the door, pushed himself up and ran past the dead body of the other gunman, Moustache, to the cell.

Sheriff Nolan and Schmidt the blacksmith were standing clutching the bars of the cell, expressions of angry frustration on their faces, which changed to ones of delight when they saw Billy Joe.

'Where's the key to the cell?' demanded Billy Joe.

'It's under that rug,' snapped Nolan. 'Jess pushed it under there.'

Billy Joe ran to the rag-rug and lifted it, revealing the key. He unlocked the door of the cell and Nolan and Schmidt hurried out and rushed to the gun rack.

'What's happening out there?' demanded Nolan.

'Shane stopped the stage before it got to the bank,' said Billy Joe. 'The soldiers are fighting off Boone's gunmen.'

'Then let's hit those varmints from a side they ain't expectin'!' said the Sheriff.

He snatched a rifle from the gun rack and ran to the door of his office. He stepped out into the street, swung the rifle up and began firing.

Schmidt had also taken a rifle from the gun rack, and he joined the Sheriff out on the boardwalk, firing at the enemy.

Billy Joe hesitated, then he reached out and selected a pistol from the gun rack. It felt heavy in his hand. He checked it for bullets. The chamber was full.

Billy Joe had only fired a gun a few times in his life, when his father tried to teach him to shoot.

'It ain't how fast you draw,' his pa had told him. 'It's how straight you shoot. Shoot straight. And aim at something big. The body. If you aim at the head or the arm you'll likely miss. You won't miss the body, not if you get close enough.'

But John Ford had only let Billy Joe fire the gun

twice. 'Bullets cost money,' he'd told Billy Joe. 'I can't afford to waste good money havin' you shoot my gun. When you can buy some bullets of your own, then you can shoot some more.'

Billy Joe held the gun in his hand and headed for the door. He peered out into the street. The Sheriff and Mr Schmidt were keeping up their firing at the gunmen. They moved nearer and nearer the scene of the gunfight, dodging behind water butts and rails to try and get some cover. They were too intent on the gunfight to notice Billy Joe.

Billy Joe took a deep breath, then ran across the Main Street to the boardwalk on the other side of the street. As he reached it, a stray bullet from the gunfight smacked into the wooden boardwalk, and he leapt to one side just in time. He fell onto the wood, hurting his elbow.

He heard a small voice saying, 'What's happening, Billy Joe?'

He looked and saw that little Andy had found shelter inside the hardware store. Billy Joe could make out Patch just behind him inside the store, as if he was hiding behind the small boy.

'You stay right there, Andy,' Billy Joe instructed the smaller boy.

Andy spotted the gun in Billy Joe's hand, 'What you gonna do with that gun?'

'I gotta deal with somethin',' replied Billy Joe.

'Can I come with you?' asked Andy eagerly.

Billy Joe shook his head.

'Nope,' he said firmly. 'You stay there and keep Patch safe. We don't want that dog gettin' loose on the street and gettin' shot.'

With that, Billy Joe got to his feet. He took one last look back at the gunfight still going on down the street, then he darted into the side alley that led to the back lane.

CHAPTER 26

Shane stayed inside the stagecoach where the soldiers had pushed him. He crouched down beneath the seats. The leather and thick wool stuffing gave him some kind of protection as the gunmen's bullets tore through the stagecoach's wood panelling.

What was happening outside? As he'd pulled the door of the stagecoach shut, he'd seen one of the soldiers crumple and fall to the ground, shot. Ever since, the shooting had continued with bullets from the gunmen hitting the stagecoach and the ground around it.

The horses had been let go almost as soon as the gun battle started. Shane had heard the soldiers shouting, and felt the thump as they'd released the harnesses from the stagecoach, then he'd heard the horses run off.

It wasn't just that the soldiers didn't want the

horses killed, the horses may have offered some cover, but they also got in the way of the soldiers as they returned fire – rearing and jumping in fear as bullets winged around them.

Cautiously, Shane pushed himself up from the floor of the stagecoach and peered out of the window of the door. He looked along the Main Street. The gunmen had found some cover on the boardwalks and behind barrels in the street. Some of them were trying to work their way along the street, going from shop to shop, to try and get nearer to the stage, but the soldiers were picking them off.

Shane saw the bodies of about six gunmen lying in the street. He wondered how many more were in the shops and out of sight?

Six gunmen dead wasn't many when he knew that Boone had about forty men. There had been ten soldiers in the cavalry escort. Shane saw that two of them, and the stagecoach driver, were dead, lying on the ground near the stage.

Shane may have managed to get the stage and cavalry to stop before they reached the bank, but they were still out in the open. Without the horses there was no chance of turning and running. They were trapped – and the gunfire from the robbers was getting stronger.

A bullet suddenly smashed into the door of the stagecoach just above Shane's head, sending a large splinter of wood into Shane's forehead. Shane dived for the floor of the stage, blood running down his face. The sound of gunfire increased.

How much longer could they hold out?

* * *

Inside the bank, Boone paced angrily, gun in hand. All but three of his men were out on the street, engaged in the gun battle with the soldiers and the stagecoach driver.

Through the shattered window of the bank he could see more of his men hiding in the wooden buildings opposite, firing.

'That damn kid!' Boone raged. He picked up a chair and threw it at the already smashed glass, causing the rest of the window to fall out into the street.

Boone fumed. It should have been so easy. Everything had gone to plan. Except for those kids. How could a bunch of kids fool a whole gang of gunmen this big? This was now gonna be one heck of a job to pull off. The stage and soldiers had stopped so far short of the bank, it was gonna be a real battle to get near them. His best hope was that the men stationed out on the roads leading into town would hear the shooting and come in to attack the soldiers from behind.

If his men in town could hold out that long . . .

Billy Joe drew near the back entrance of the bank. He saw the back door open and a man hurry out. Billy Joe stopped and shrank back, but then he saw it was Mayor Redding.

The Mayor had taken advantage of everyone's attention being on the gunfight to sneak out of his office and run for the back door. The man stopped to make sure no gunmen were watching him, and then he ran, his head down and his legs going as fast as they could carry him. He was heading in the direction of the livery stable. Billy Joe guessed he was going to grab a horse and get as far away as he could.

The good thing was that if Mayor Redding had been able to get out of the bank by the back door, then it was likely there was no one in there keeping guard on it.

Billy Joe hurried to the back door of the bank. When he got there, he stopped and listened. He could hear shouting from inside. Boone's harsh voice, giving instructions to his men.

Billy Joe held the butt of the pistol in his right hand and cradled the barrel in his left. It sure felt heavy. He felt sick to his stomach at what he was going to do.

He slipped in through the door and crept along the corridor that led to the main room of the bank. The door to the main room was half open. The sound of firing from inside the bank and outside was deafening.

Billy Joe tilted back the brim of his hat and carefully pushed the door open a little wider.

There were only four gunmen inside the bank. Three of them were crouched by the shattered window, shooting at the soldiers outside.

The fourth, Boone, stood back from the window, both guns drawn, shouting angrily. His back was to Billy Joe.

'I want every one of those soldiers dead!' Boone raged. 'I came here for that gold and there ain't nothin' gonna stop me! Keep firing! Keep 'em stuck by that stage!'

Billy Joe held his breath as he raised the gun with both hands. He pointed it straight at Boone's back. He knew he had just one shot to end all this. Once he fired, the other gunmen would turn on him. He daren't step any further into the room to make sure of his aim because that would mean he'd have too far to run to get away.

Billy Joe aimed the gun and began to tighten his finger on the trigger.

He remembered his father's instructions, 'Squeeze it gentle, don't pull on it! If you pull it sharp the gun's just gonna jump in your hand and the bullet can go anywhere. Squeeze the trigger slow.'

Billy Joe squeezed the trigger, but it was too strong for him. It wouldn't pull! He tried harder, using both first fingers together, pulling as slow but as hard as he could . . . and as he did so, Boone must have felt someone was behind him, because he began to move.

Boone turned and looked at Billy Joe. The shock on his face changed to one of extreme anger, and he swung his gun to aim at Billy Joe.

BANG!

The gun jumped in Billy Joe's hand as he fired and the bullet hit Boone straight in the face, right between the eyes.

At the sound of the shot the three gunmen turned, but Billy Joe was already running down the corridor to the back door, then out into the back lane. Behind him he heard frantic yells of 'Boone's dead!' and 'Get that kid!'

Billy Joe ran as fast as he could, his chest hurting from the air being forced out of his lungs as he ran. At any moment he expected to hear a gun fire and feel a bullet in his back. He came to the first alley that led back to the Main Street. He ducked inside it and leant against the wood of the nearest building. He was shaking. The gun felt really heavy in his hand, so heavy he thought he might drop it. Instead, he wrapped his fingers tighter around its butt.

He'd shot and killed a man. Shot him right between the eyes at point blank range. He had to be dead. There was no way Boone was coming back from that, coming after him. Was there?

Once more, Billy Joe felt sick. Not because of what he'd just done, but from fear that Boone wasn't dead. That he'd be coming after Billy Joe.

Billy Joe fought to keep the nausea down.

He had to find the others.

Jess was in the saloon, shot. Shane was out on the street, caught up in the middle of the gunfight. Andy was in the hardware store with Patch. Or, at least, he would be, providing he'd obeyed Billy Joe's order to stay there. But little Andy seemed to do things when he wanted to, regardless of what anyone told him. Like the way he'd just run along the Main Street with Patch and nearly got himself shot.

Billy Joe took a lot of deep breaths and gradually got his shaking under control.

He wondered how the gunfight was going on. Were the soldiers winning? What had happened to the Sheriff and Mr Schmidt?

What about the other gunmen hidden in the other buildings? What about the townsfolk in the saloon?

Billy Joe edged along the alley towards the Main Street, the gun heavy but firm in his hand. If he saw any of the gunmen on his way he was gonna kill them. But, most of all, he was gonna stay alive and survive this.

Shane touched his forehead. It ached, but it had stopped bleeding. He could feel the blood clotting stickily all down his face. From outside the stage he heard a yell of pain, then a thump as another soldier crashed backwards into the stagecoach and slid down it. Another soldier dead or wounded.

Suddenly he heard a voice shouting. 'Boone's dead! Boone's dead!' Then the shouting vanished in a burst of gunfire.

Boone was dead! Shane felt a huge feeling of excitement and elation.

All at once, Shane heard a different sound above the noise of the gunfire. It was the sound of a bugle. And the sound of horses' hooves thundering nearer. Were the soldiers' horses coming back?

Once more Shane forced himself up from the floor and looked out of the window of the stagecoach, towards the edge of town, to see a cavalry banner approaching. There were more soldiers coming! Lots more!

CHAPTER 27

As Shane watched, the reinforcements swept into town, hooves drumming on the road, the soldiers firing from their saddles, pouring hot lead into the gunmen on the boardwalks and on the street. There had to be at least twenty more soldiers arriving!

The gunmen who were still standing were starting to surrender, throwing down their guns and standing up with their hands in the air. First it was just one or two, then more joined in. They knew they were now the outnumbered ones and that if they surrendered there was a chance they could go to jail. If they resisted, most of them knew they'd die for sure.

'Hold your fire!' called out one of the soldiers.

The bugle sounded again, its call much louder than the yelled command. The soldiers stopped firing but kept their rifles and pistols trained on the gunmen in the street.

Shane now saw that the soldier who'd shouted the order to stop firing was an officer, with stripes and badges on his sleeves.

A captain.

The man rode towards the bank, soldiers flanking him on either side, their guns ready to fire.

'All of you men come out with your hands up!' called the Captain. 'I promise you'll get a fair trial. Any man who tries to fight will get shot here and now. This is your chance to stay alive.'

The doors of the buildings opened and men shuffled out, their hands held up in the air, to join their companions who were already standing on the street, hands held high.

Shane reckoned there must only be about twenty of the gunmen left alive. The bodies of the others were sprawled in the dust of the Main Street, and on the boardwalk, or hanging over the wooden tethering rail. He guessed that some of the gunmen, especially those guarding the roads at the edge of town, had managed to get away.

As the silence filled the air, and Shane realized the gunfighting really was over, he pushed open the door of the stagecoach and climbed down onto the street. He wondered how the rest of the boys were? Was Jess still alive? Had Billy Joe and Andy managed to get under cover?

He started to walk along the main street, heading

for the saloon to see how Jess was, but a soldier stopped him.

'Stay with the stage for the moment, son,' he said. 'Let's get these varmints safely chained up first before you start walking around. We don't want to give 'em a chance of trying something.'

Shane hesitated, then nodded. He went back to the stage and sat down on its step. Townsfolk had started to appear from the saloon, but soldiers were ordering them back inside, off the street for their own safety.

Shane looked around him: at the soldiers on horseback, at the others ordering the gunmen to stand in line, and at the dead bodies of soldiers and gunmen lying in the street.

It was all over.

It took hours for the last of the gunmen to be rounded up. They were taken to the blacksmith's forge under armed guard, where Schmidt shackled the gunmen together in groups of four with heavy chains and manacles around their ankles.

The town was coming alive now, people hurrying to and fro. Some were nailing boards across broken and shattered windows. Others were checking their neighbours were unharmed.

In the saloon Jess was lying on the floor and being

attended by Preacher Varley, when Sheriff Nolan and the army Captain walked in. Billy Joe, Shane, Andy and Patch were also in the saloon, as were Mr and Mrs Johnson and Priscilla, all looking on anxiously as Jess bit his lip to stop himself yelling out with the pain. Varley finished fixing a splint to Jess's injured leg and got to his feet.

'There,' he said. 'It's rough, it but it'll hold until Doc Benson gets back. The main thing is there ain't no infection in the wound.' He smiled at Mrs Johnson. 'Thanks to your quick thinking, m'am.'

Nolan looked at the repair job and the bandages.

'If you ask me, it looks as neat a job as I ever saw Doc Benson do, Mr Varley,' he murmured. 'I didn't know you was a medical man.'

The preacher gave a shrug.

'In the War, we all had to be medical men, Sheriff,' he said. He looked at his wife and children standing, waiting and watching. 'Right, family. I suggest we return to our home and leave the Sheriff and the Captain to deal with things here.' He nodded politely to the Sheriff and Captain, and the Johnsons. 'Good-day,' he said.

With that, the Varley family made their exit, the Preacher and his wife first, their seven children trailing behind like ducklings.

'I guess we better get home now as well,' said Mr Johnson.

'You go home with Priscilla, Amos,' said Mrs Johnson. 'And start preparing a bed for young Jess.'

'No,' Jess tried to protest, but his voice was weak and feeble.

'Yes!' said Mrs Johnson firmly. 'You ain't staying at that tumbledown shack of yours while you've only got one good leg. You need nursing and being kept clean'.'

'We can do that,' piped up Andy.

Mrs Johnson looked down at little Andy and smiled.

'Andy, you can't even keep yourself properly clean. But don't worry, once Jess is over the worst we'll have him back to you.' To her husband, she said, 'Go on now, Amos, and send Priscilla back here when the place is ready.' Turning to the Sheriff, she added, 'I'm sure the Sheriff can arrange some strong men to get Jess to our house.'

'You can be sure of that, ma'am,' said Nolan.

Amos and Priscilla Johnson nodded politely, and then left. Mrs Johnson bent over Jess.

'How's the pain?' she asked him. She held the whiskey bottle up. 'You want any more of this here stuff to dull it?'

Jess shook his head.

'No thank you, Mrs Johnson,' he said. 'To be honest, it makes me feel a little sick in the stomach.'

Nolan stepped forward.

'Jess,' he said. 'This here's Captain Oakes from the army. He wants to meet you.'

Jess looked up at the tall figure of the army captain.
'Sir?' he asked.

Oakes smiled.

'I want to meet the brave young man who stopped more of my men from being killed,' he said.

'That weren't him,' spoke up Billy Joe. 'That was Shane who ran out in the road and warned 'em. He was the brave one.'

Sheriff Nolan turned to Shane, whose face had flushed red with embarrassment.

'I think what the Captain means is he wanted to meet all of you,' he said. 'After all, Jess got shot trying to spring me from jail. He could've been killed. You could've been killed running out in that road, Shane.'

'Me and Patch could've been killed when we were out on the street,' added Andy. 'And Billy Joe could've been killed when he ran into the bank.'

Sheriff Nolan and Captain Oakes turned to look at Billy Joe, surprise on their faces.

'You went into in the bank?' asked Nolan.

Billy Joe's head was in a whirl. He'd shot Boone, but he'd done it in the back. Well, not exactly the back, because Boone had turned round. But he'd tried to shoot him in the back. Was that murder? Was the Sheriff going to arrest him?

'No . . .' began Billy Joe awkwardly.

'Yes he did,' insisted Andy. 'Billy Joe told me to stay with Patch in Mr Pantages' hardware store, but I crept out to see if he needed help.' He smiled at Billy proudly. 'You was holding that pistol, remember, Billy Joe. You went in there the back way to fight those gunmen!'

Billy Joe felt his mouth open and close helplessly. Andy had followed him!

Captain Oakes walked over to Billy Joe and put his hand on his shoulder.

'Young man,' he said, 'I don't know whether to shout at you for being so foolish, or congratulate you for doing one of the bravest things I ever heard. To go in alone against armed gunmen . . .'

Billy Joe shook his head.

'I wasn't thinking clearly,' he stammered. 'I don't know what I was doin'.' Then, desperate to change the subject, he said to the Captain: 'But how come you arrived with reinforcements like you did? Boone had this town cut off!'

'The telegraph office at River Creek got the start of a message from Drygulch, but then it got cut off,' said the Captain. 'They knew the shipment of gold was coming here today, so they suspected maybe something was wrong. A cavalry detachment was sent to try and catch up with the stage and escort. Luckily, we arrived just in time.'

'M-my message g-got through!' said Shane delightedly.

The Captain looked at Shane in surprise.

'That was you?' he asked.

'Yes, s-sir,' said Shane. 'I st-started to send a message, but this g-gunman came in and . . .' Shane's voice faltered, then he said, '. . . and he sh-shot my b-brother P-Pete. And I ran out. But I d-didn't think I'd s-sent the wire.'

'You did,' confirmed the Captain. 'Only the start of it, but it was enough.'

He turned and looked at Sheriff Nolan.

'It seems to me you must be very proud of these young men, Sheriff, and what they did today. If it hadn't been for them . . .'

He was interrupted by the sound of running boots outside and the bat-wing doors swinging open, as the Mayor burst in.

'Thank heavens!' cried the Mayor. He stomped over to Captain Oakes, hand held out. He took hold of the Captain's hand and began to pump it up and down heartily.

'Mayor Redding,' he introduced himself. 'Also, owner of the local bank. On behalf of the town, I thank you, Captain, for your bravery here today in saving the people of Drygulch! I would have been here before, but I've been busy trying to get help myself!'

'Oh yeah?' sneered Billy Joe. 'You were hiding!'

The Mayor turned on Billy Joe with a scowl and looked as if he was about to snarl at the boy, but he stopped himself as he saw the expressions on the faces of the Captain and the Sheriff, and Mrs Johnson.

'Of course I was hiding,' he said, forcing a smile. 'That was part of my plan to defeat these villains!'

'Yes, well, Mr Mayor, I guess we'll leave you sort out details with Captain Oakes here,' said Nolan. 'I'll take these boys back to their home. I understand those gunmen did some damage to it.'

'They shot it up,' said Billy Joe.

'Then let's take a walk over there and see just what needs doing to fix it up,' said Nolan. To Mrs Johnson, he said, 'I'll be back shortly with some strong men and a buckboard, Mrs Johnson, and we'll get Jess moved to your house.'

'That would be appreciated, Sheriff,' smiled Mrs Johnson.

Nolan headed for the door of the saloon. The boys went to Jess. Billy Joe took off the hat Jess had given him that morning and placed it on Jess's chest.

'Guess I won't need this for a disguise no more,' he said.

Jess reached down and touched his father's old Stetson fondly, and smiled.

'It sure did good when we needed it, though,' the older boy said.

'It sure did,' agreed Billy Joe.

Jess lifted the hat up and held it out to Billy Joe.

'Tell you what, why don't you hang on to it for the moment,' he said. 'You wear it.'

'But it's your pa's hat,' Billy Joe pointed out. But he

was aware that something special was happening here with Jess's offer, something good.

'Yeah, but I got his watch. You got nothin' of your pa's. So why don't we share this hat, till I get me a new one.'

Billy Joe felt his heart filling up. In all his life he'd never known what it was to be part of a family. Not a real family. Now he knew. He nodded gratefully. He took the hat and put it on.

'Thanks, Jess,' he said. 'I'll take good care of it.'

'I know you will,' smiled Jess.

The sound of boots on the wooden floor made them turn. Sheriff Nolan had returned, with four men.

'OK, Jess,' he said. 'The buckboard's outside, and there's some men here who'll carry you out to it.'

'W-we'll come and see you l-later, Jess,' said Shane. 'Once you're settled in.'

'Make sure you do,' said Mrs Johnson. 'If you come in about an hour, it'll be suppertime.'

'You mean we can come for supper?' asked Andy eagerly.

'Andy!' said Shane, disapprovingly. 'We never b-beg, you know that.'

'I wasn't begging. I was just asking,' said Andy.

'And in this case, it's not begging, it's called hospitality,' said Mrs Johnson. 'I'll see you all in an hour.' She looked at the Sheriff and smiled. 'You too, Sheriff, if you're free.'

'Thank you, ma'am, I'd appreciate that,' said the Sheriff.

The boys and Nolan waved goodbye to Jess, and headed for the door, Patch following them, his tail wagging. The men Nolan had brought went to Jess, and started getting ready to carry him out to the waiting buckboard. Mayor Redding was still talking to the army captain, assuring him of his assistance in making sure these bandits paid for their crime in any way that he, the Mayor, could help.

As they stepped out into the street, Shane said suddenly to Nolan, 'My b-brother P-Pete needs to be b-buried p-proper. In a p-p-proper grave and a s-service an' all. He was a h-hero. He needs a p-proper hero's grave.'

Nolan nodded.

'I agree,' he said sadly. 'Leave it to me to organize, Shane. I'll make sure the townsfolk put up the money for a proper funeral and a proper headstone. I know they'll be happy to do that.' He gave a smile. 'And I'll make sure that Mayor Redding puts the biggest amount of money towards it.'

The boys and Patch the dog walked along beside the Sheriff, heading down a side alley towards their shack.

'I hear that someone shot Boone,' said Sheriff.

'Sh-shot him?' echoed Shane. Billy Joe stayed quiet.

The Sheriff nodded once more.

'Right between the eyes,' he said. 'They found his body in the bank.'

'Who d-did it?' asked Shane.

'No one knows,' said Nolan. 'But it strikes me it's gotta be someone who's real good with a gun to shoot a man like Boone face to face right between the eyes.' He looked pointedly at Billy Joe. 'That means, it's gotta be someone older. Someone who knows how to handle a gun. And whoever it was, it all happened during a gunfight, so there's no blame on whoever did it. You hear what I'm saying, Billy Joe?'

Billy Joe nodded, but kept his eyes looking down on the ground as they walked.

'I tell you one thing, though,' added the Sheriff. 'It must've taken a lot of courage to go in and face up to Boone like that, whoever it was. Boone being the killer he was, an' all. Someone brave like that would be good to have around this town. If he felt like stayin', he'd be more than welcome.'

Billy Joe said nothing.

He walked along, heading towards the shack. Shane walked beside Billy Joe, a proud look in his eyes at the realization that he had managed to send the telegraph wire after all. Little Andy skipped along in front of them, now and then grabbing Patch by the ears or the tail and scratching the dog.

The shack would be a mess, but they could fix it up. And Jess would be up and about soon enough.

Billy Joe thought of his father, John Ford. Less than twenty-four hours before his pa had been alive. Now he was dead. And so was the man who'd shot him. What was it Boone had said when he'd been looking for Billy Joe on that dreadful night?

'I'm just making sure he don't come back and shoot me in the back. It's what I did to the man who killed my pa.'

The boy could remember the other man saying that Billy Joe hadn't looked the killing kind, and he remembered Boone's answer:

'Everyone's the killing kind. Remember that.'

It seemed Boone had got one thing right.

Rest in peace, *Pa*, thought Billy Joe.

BADLANDS
RANGE WARS

'Get your hands in the air! Keep your guns on 'em, men! If they move, shoot 'em!'

The boys stared in shock at the man in the light brown suit and the two cowboys holding pistols pointed at them.

'What's goin' on?' demanded Jess angrily. 'We ain't done nothin'!'

When the Drygulch gang are thrown out of the shack they call home, they have to move on – but they soon find themselves caught up in a deadly range war . . .

SECOND IN THE EXCITING BADLANDS SERIES BY
ELDRIDGE JAMES

For more information about Badlands
or to find out more about other great
Catnip titles go to:

www.catnippublishing.co.uk